PURE DYNASTY IV

Pure Dynasty IV

LEILA ALMARZOH

Leila Almarzoh

Copyright © 2021 by Leila Almarzoh

All rights reserved. No part of this book may be reproduced in any manner whatsoever without written permission except in the case of brief quotations embodied in critical articles and reviews.

First Printing, 2021

CONTENTS

~ 1 ~
Thanksgiving Dinner
1

~ 2 ~
Vibrations
15

~ 3 ~
The Sun Witch
29

~ 4 ~
Left Behind
42

~ 5 ~
Moon Power
53

~ 6 ~
Wicca
64

~ 7 ~
Parallel Universe
79

~ 8 ~
Voodooism
94

~ 9 ~
Freedom
110

~ 10 ~
Destined
122

~ 11 ~
The Magic School Bus
132

~ 12 ~
Endurance
143

~ 13 ~
Resurrection
157

~ 14 ~
The Star Witch
173

~ 15 ~

Understanding

187

~ 16 ~

Do-over

201

~ 17 ~

Heaven

218

~ 18 ~

The Beginning Of The End

229

~ 19 ~

Divided Together

243

~ 20 ~

What's Next

255

~ 1 ~

THANKSGIVING DINNER

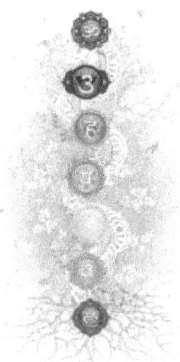

The house was quiet, and time seemed to be moving slowly on the morning of Thanksgiving, November 24, 2022. From the windows, the sound of birds chirping could be heard as they chatted on the roof. Isabel was in bed, and as she opened her eyes, a single bird sat on the edge of her window. She fixed her gaze on the bird without moving, and after a few seconds, the bird suddenly vanished.

Upon hearing the bird on the ledge of her other window, Isabel leapt to her feet. She turned to look at it but once again, he disappeared and reappeared right in front of her eyes.

Immediately after the bird left, Isabel ran to Ladle's room and woke her. She explained what she'd seen.

"Maybe the bird just flew quickly, dear, to the other side or another one came," Ladle said, still half asleep.

"I was staring at it. My eyes were glued to him, and I saw it there and then bam gone. Not fly away, but just disappear then reappear on the other side," Isabel explained.

Ladle wasn't sure what to think. Rubbing her eyes and sitting up, she told Isabel planet Earth didn't have enchantment unless a witch caused it.

"So someone is causing this?" Isabel asked.

Ladle walked and looked out Isabel's
Window, wrapping her robe around her. She stood at the window but didn't see anyone or anything.

She shrugged her shoulders and told her if
she noticed anything else to let her know, but for now,
they had to get ready. Ladle was preparing a
Thanksgiving dinner that night and inviting everyone.
Not only to come together and have a good time, but the plan was to invite Sef and find out more about the Sun Witch.

Tulin had told Ladle that Sef always stayed in the university's basement, never once having a family member come to visit him or even talk about his family. Once in a while, Tulin would ask him family questions, but Sef always gave quick answers and never revealed too much. Altair didn't celebrate Thanksgiving, so Ladle thought a big family meal was just what Sef needed to open up.

Rene tried to talk to Sef, but he kept saying he didn't remember the Sun Witch. Even in Rene's dreams, she couldn't get him to open up, and she knew he was lying. Every time she dreamed of him, it seemed to end with him magically removing his mouth and telling Rene through his mind that he didn't remember, as if he was the one controlling her dreams.

He knew something, but for some reason, he wouldn't talk about it, even if it meant seeing James again.

Molly sat in bed listening to Ladle and Isabel walk past her room heading downstairs. She rolled over and grabbed her phone from the nightstand to see if Danny had texted her. There was no missed call or text. She shook her head, thinking to herself, *Why would he send a simple text now that he knows who he is and what he is capable of doing?* Who knew if he would even text anymore. Molly figured maybe that was just too human for him to do. Thinking too much, she sat up and took a deep breath.

It was going to be another day without Danny. Molly glanced out the window as she walked to her door and saw clouds in the sky.

Stop looking at your phone; he will return when he's ready, it read. As Molly read the words, they faded away.

Even though it was cute, Molly felt like Beyron was watching. She smiled and closed her shades. Molly walked downstairs as Isabel and Ladle were cleaning up and already cooking for dinner that night. When Isabel saw Molly, she told her that Angela wouldn't make it tonight because she needed to be with her mom and Danny's dad.

Even though they kept telling their parents Danny would be back soon, Angela felt horrible knowing it was a spell they were under and Danny would be missing Thanksgiving. Molly nodded, grabbing a plain bagel and tossing it into the toaster oven.

"Between Dad and Danny, this isn't going to be as wonderful a Thanksgiving as you guys might think," Molly said.

"You think we don't know that? We are just trying to get everyone together after everything we have been through. We deserve a normal dinner," Isabel yelled out.

"Oh, please. It's all to gang up on Sef and beg him for information. We are moon witches. We can get it out of him if we use our crescent power," Molly said.

"Molly, stop," Ladle said as she walked into the kitchen from cleaning up the living room. "Of course, we need information, but that's not all that this dinner is about. Abigor, Lord Amir, Abraxas, the other side, the prophecy, vampires, wolves, and the list goes on and on.

"We need to come together and talk about what we could do to keep this planet safe and hopefully, yes, get that information to see your father even for a moment," Ladle said as one single tear fell down her face and onto the ground. The room was silent for a single second when the toaster oven beeped, and Molly jumped from the noise.

She pulled out her bagel as Isabel gave her the cream cheese. "I get it," Molly said grabbing the cream cheese and sitting down at the table. Austin walked down the stairs. Ladle continued to clean up the living room as Isabel took out the cereal and milk for Austin.

***

Broomsticks were flying above Altair as Anthony and Corbin rode through the skies. It was a race to see who could ride the fastest when Tulin came out of the building. When Anthony saw him, he stopped short. Corbin didn't know and kept going. He laughed because he thought he was finally ahead of Anthony.

When he looked back, he saw Anthony had stopped and was flying back down toward Tulin. Corbin turned again in front of him just in time. He stopped a few centimeters from the tall building.

Tulin told them they shouldn't be playing around like that. They needed to go back to class. Looking at Anthony, Tulin said when he graduated, the university would require him to become the Magic Knight's leader.

Anthony knew the university was only two years, and then he could be a leader of the knights himself. So he had some time to think if that was what he wanted to do. When they graduated from the university, they chose the path they decided to go on, and there was no turning back when becoming the leader of the knights.

You learned what you were capable of doing while you were there, but once the two years were up, you had a duty to follow the path you were destined for Every witch came with their own ability. With that ability, there was a responsibility, and Anthony was a warrior.

He had to defend the planet because his strength was the key to the war against evil.

Rene's path was to help their future and guide those who needed to find their path. Rene was already using her power for that because she didn't want to let her father down. She was in Herbs class learning the magic in different flowers, seasoning, and herbs that made up the spells in every spell book. When Patricia walked up to Rene and thanked her for dreaming of her mother and bringing them together again, Rene told Patricia it wasn't a problem.

She was happy to help. Patricia walked away with a smile as Vannessa asked Rene in a whisper, what if she changed something in the future by helping Patricia, and she wasn't supposed to find her mother again? Rene smiled and told her if it was a fixed point

in time, it couldn't be changed, but the dreams she had been having recently showed more in-depth than ever before. She knew what paths could and should be changed.

"So do you know the direction or path everyone is supposed to be on or something? And like all the moments that come with it?" Vannessa asked.

Rene smiled. "My dreams do tell me everything but not all at once. So I can't really pick and choose what I see unless there is some sort of spell, like I've seen before, one that helps me find it. If I see it in this 3D world, I will eventually dream about it and when I'm able to, I can make changes that I am meant to make.

Astonished, Vannessa shook her head in amazement, thinking the universe had a plan and everyone had a purpose. Finding it was something Rene could see in her dreams.

After class, Vannessa and Rene walked to their building. They saw Sef walking toward the fire building. Rene told Vannessa she would meet her inside. She wanted to talk to Sef again and invite him to the dinner. Vannessa nodded and continued walking. Rene looked at Sef wondering to herself, *Why can't I get his memory of the Sun Witch out of him even when I'm dreaming?*

Rene knew Sef had the ability to talk to the gods and find out what element every witch was in Altair but going into her dreams and controlling them wasn't something everyone knew about him. Rene walked toward Sef.

"Excuse me! Sef!" Rene yelled out as she ran toward him. "Please, stop walking!" Rene continued to yell out, but Sef wasn't stopping. "Sef!"

Finally, he stopped. "Yes, may I help you with something?" Sef asked looking behind him.

"I'm not here to ask about the Sun Witch again even though I still don't understand why you won't speak about her," Rene said as she began to catch her breath. "My mother is having a big family dinner at our house. We want you to come. Everyone will be there, including me and Anthony's coven." Sef looked away as if he was thinking. Rene noticed the hesitation. "It's for family and friends, Sef. Tulin told us you were close with my father; you should be there."

"I can't. I'm sorry. I have work to do," Sef said as he walked away.

"Seriously? First, you control my dreams, and now, you won't be there for my grieving mother? My father was your friend. I heard stories about you two. How could you not give us anything, not even a dinner?" Rene screamed as Sef continued to walk away. "You look suspicious right now, Sef, and now you know we are determined to find out why!" Rene screamed as students walked past, staring at her.

Sef walked into the fire building. Rene ran to find Anthony. She told him what had just happened. Anthony looked toward his building and smirked. Rene asked why he was smiling when now they had to tell Ladle he wasn't coming.

Anthony said he wasn't laughing. He told Rene Sef wanted them to find out. He knew very well their family wouldn't stop until they understood. She shook her head and asked why the hell he couldn't just tell them. Anthony shrugged his shoulders and told her maybe Sef couldn't, and that was why he wanted them to look for the answers elsewhere.

Rene stayed quiet for a couple of seconds
while she was thinking. Anthony said the reason Sef

couldn't was a mystery. It was something they would have to figure out on their own. They stood at a distance, watching Sef walk out of the fire building and into his shed.

***

Hours passed on Earth, and Ladle was putting the last touches on the dinner table. The house was clean, and the food was ready. Isabel walked down the stairs in a long forest-green dress that hugged her waist. Ladle took one look at her and smiled.

She told Isabel she looked beautiful. Isabel smiled back. Molly came down the stairs with her red hair dyed back. She shocked Ladle and Isabel. Molly smirked and told them to take a picture, it would last longer as she grabbed another roll on the table and stuffed it into her mouth. Isabel and Ladle looked at each other, laughing.

"We just can't believe your hair is back to red. Why? Don't get me wrong, it's beautiful, but why?" Isabel asked.

"I'm sick of keeping it black. Maybe one day I'll try another color, but right now, I want this one. That's all," Molly said as Ladle squeezed Molly's shoulder with a smile on her face.

"Well, you look wonderful," Ladle said.

Austin came down the stairs and heard the real reason Molly did that. The reason was James, he always brushed her hair with his fingers when she was little. This was not from what she remembered because she was too young, but Austin heard in Molly's mind that she went back in time just to see James with her as a child. He put her to sleep when she was little, and while brushing her hair, he said she was going to have the most beautiful long red hair just like his grandmother had as he kissed her and said goodnight.

Austin walked past Molly looking at her and said her hair was beautiful, and she looked like part of the family again. Molly rolled her eyes because she knew Austin saw her memory.

"Says the one with brown hair. Like, can't you turn it off? It's been how long? You know how to control it. So turn it off and stop always listening," Molly said in a whisper walking to the living room.

Austin grabbed a bottle of water and took a deep breath. He wasn't like his siblings. They could control their abilities now, but Austin had trouble turning it off completely. As he took a deep breath, he drank the water and used his mind to turn it off, then walked toward Ladle. He couldn't hear her thoughts. He smiled, knowing it worked. Sometimes, it would turn off, but then it came back by itself. Austin still felt like it was not all controllable.

Molly was putting some thick dark eyeliner on, and Isabel sprayed perfume on herself as the first bell began to ring. Ladle opened the door, and it was Beyron, Anthony, and his whole coven. As the night continued, everyone was coming—Rene, Vannessa, their coven, Tulin, Bobbie, some of the witches, Blair, and Doug. Clara, Amanda, and some of the wolves showed up at the same time.

Finn was next with two vampires by his side. As Shelby rang the bell, the siblings looked at each other. Ladle welcomed her and told her children she wasn't who she used to be ever since she met Gastle and experienced the other side.

When Serenity came, Anthony had no idea she was coming or was able to get to planet Earth. Rene smiled and asked Anthony if he knew what Tulin's ability was.

Anthony shrugged his shoulders and answered, "Strength?"

Rene smiled and told him he made the seeds to travel through planets. Tulin smiled and closed his fist tight, and when he opened it, a seed popped out. Ladle smiled and told them he was the one her parents would go to get the seeds, and that was how she got here all those years ago. The seeds created a magic tree, letting them travel to each planet. Anthony smiled at Serenity as she smiled back from across the room.

Rene whispered in Anthony's ear. "When I dreamed of us on planet Mars in our other life. I found something out about who your soulmate was."

Anthony looked at Rene and then at Serenity. He shook his head and walked quickly out the door and into the backyard. Rene was confused about why he looked upset. Ladle walked up to Rene when she saw Anthony walk out. She asked what happened, and when Rene told her. Ladle knew Anthony was upset. Serenity was not from Altair. She had a duty as the ocean god's daughter to stay in Kepler and fight for their world, and Anthony had the same obligation for Altair. So they could not be together if the planets they had to protect weren't the same.

Just as everyone was gathering around the table, the doorbell rang again. Rene and Ladle looked at each other, hoping it was Sef. When Anthony opened the door, it was Brenda and her father. Ladle smiled as they too were invited. Austin looked at her in shock. Molly started cracking up.

She told Ladle, "Way to go making this an awkward party between Serenity and now Brenda." Molly asked if Ryan was coming too. Ladle told her "no" only because of the breakup. Isabel overheard. Raising her voice across the room, she told Molly to stop, knowing if he had come, it would have been hard to stay away from him. Ladle knew that already, and that was why she sent Cassie a message to apologize and to make up a time when they would get together again.

Everyone gathered around the table. Ladle thanked everyone for coming and told them James would have loved to be there with all of them today. She continued to talk about how everyone there had helped her family somehow, and she was thankful for that. Just as everyone was about to dig in, Isabel stood up and had a question for all the magical beings at that dinner table. Ladle had told them they should all help planet Earth stay safe and away from the threats in the universe. So Isabel's question was why? Why did humans need to be protected? Were they weak, or was there another reason that no one was talking about?

Everyone looked at each other. Then looked at Doug as he was the only human at that table. Suddenly, a low knock came from the door. Everyone looked toward it. Ladle looked at her children. Isabel walked to open the door as everyone was eager to look.

It was Angela. She seemed out of breath. Isabel let her inside as everyone looked at her. Angela said hi to everyone, and Isabel asked what was wrong.

She told them she was at her grandmother's for Thanksgiving, and she found some papers that were her father's. Some didn't make sense to her, but then she saw something that caught her attention. Angela held it up. It was a piece of ripped-up paper. On it was a map of a mountain. Mount Shasta, to be exact. Isabel shook her head as she knew Angela's father had gone there already.

Angela smiled and told her, "No, it's not just a map of the mountain. Look what he wrote in small words here near the mountain."

Isabel grabbed the paper and looked at what Angela's father wrote, and she read it aloud. "Inside the mountain is the brightest witch. The door to the parallel universe." Isabel read as everyone's mouth was open in shock.

"That's not all," Angela said as she handed Isabel another piece of paper. "And this one."

"The healer's touch will break the spell," Isabel read out loud.

Everyone looked at each other. Ladle held her mouth in shock. Angela told them he was writing things that didn't make sense, but what did was the map to the door of the parallel universe and the key, which was Isabel.

~ 2 ~

VIBRATIONS

The following day, the siblings head back to Mount Shasta in California, but this time Angela went along to see if she could finally see her father.

Angela considered that maybe he was onto something with his fascination for the mountain's stories, despite everyone else thinking he had gone crazy and wanted nothing to do with his daughter.

When they arrived, they saw how many spiritual seekers were there, and they needed to get closer to the mountain. As they were walking a few feet away, a lady stopped them and told them it was a volcano and they shouldn't go any closer. Molly told her they had been on the mountain before and that they would be fine. The lady smiled and replied it was more than a volcano as she looked at Isabel and touched her hand.

Everyone looked confused, and Isabel politely pulled away. Rene told the lady they would be fine and if there was something else she needed. The lady shook her head and told them they would see

for themselves as she walked away.

They looked at Austin, and Anthony asked what the lady was thinking. Austin couldn't hear anything because he felt like his ability was still off. He told them he'd keep trying, but he couldn't hear anything right now. Anthony shook his head in disappointment.

He told Austin to breathe and use his mind to open it up and channel his power. They walked closer to the mountain, and right when Austin touched the peak with his foot, his mind opened up.

All the siblings felt different, as if the mountain did have a higher frequency and opened their minds and abilities. Molly told them that she sensed a strong vibration even before when they were on top of the mountain. Isabel touched the mountain, hoping to open it, but nothing happened. She asked Angela to see the papers again. They looked and still couldn't understand what spell she could use to break open the mountain and find the brightest witch who they believed was the Sun Witch.

They walked all around. Isabel touched everywhere, but nothing was happening. Molly told them she tried going back to the moment Sef met the Sun Witch, but she couldn't. Now that she felt stronger just by standing close to the mountain, she thought they should use the crescent power.

They all agreed. They knew this Mountain was their lead, but Isabel's touch did not open it. The siblings held hands. First, they shielded themselves so no one could see them or hear them. Angela waited as she asked around if anyone knew the story behind this mountain. The siblings were going around and around, trying to hold onto each other. Colors were spinning, and their bodies felt like they were being sucked into a portal but then the movement all stopped.

They all tried to open their eyes but couldn't. Their voices echoed as sound waves vibrated through their bodies. They couldn't get out of the portal. After what seemed like seconds, they finally let go. When they felt their feet back on the ground, they could open their eyes. Angela was staring at them with a man and woman by her side. Molly was panicking as everyone else was holding their head in pure dizziness. They realized they hadn't gone anywhere.

Molly told them that never happened to her. They were being blocked from going ultimately through. She tried again, but she couldn't even get to that portal-looking thing. Isabel, still out of breath and in shock, asked Angela who the people she was standing next to were.

The man and woman were sister and brother, and they couldn't believe what they had just seen. Seeing the siblings appear like that, they were ecstatic.

"He was right. He is right!" the woman said, laughing and softly pushing her brother. "Holy crap, did you see that?"

"Who was right and who are you guys?" Austin asked.

"This is Cole, and this is Lucy. They know about the mountain and know a couple who have been studying this mountain for years after they found a spell book up at the top of the mountain," Angela explained.

"We sure do. The man calls himself Salman and his wife, Chava. They know everything, and Salman has his own followers. He shares his experience with the magical beings who have come out of this mountain," Cole said.

"He talks about how the Earth shifts and when it does a vibration pours out of the mountain and could evolve a human being into a universal entity," Lucy explained.

Anthony asked what a universal entity was. Cole and Lucy shrugged their shoulders and looked at each other. Lucy told them they weren't sure, but Salman said it gave power to humans. The siblings looked at each other in confusion. Isabel told them there was something about humans that even Hecate would keep hidden and safe. Angela asked Isabel if Hecate was once them, wouldn't they know the secret?

Rene answered she had tried every meditation possible, and she couldn't remember. Cole looked at his sister and told them maybe they needed to go into the state of Sadhana.

Anthony had heard that before from his father. He asked if that was also meditation. Lucy nodded but told him it was of a different kind, and Salman could teach them how. Molly told them to lead the way because they needed to meet this man and find more answers. The brother and sister agreed and told them to follow but to be aware, they lived in a forest, and the animals were very territorial and kept their house safe from everyone.

Rene asked how animals would do that without power. Cole said animals had more power than they thought. Isabel remembered the bird from the morning.

Austin asked how they would get in then. Lucy shrugged her shoulders as Cole smiled. She replied that the couple would just feel their energy and hear them from a mile away.

They walked through trees all around and sticks that stood up, making a triangle higher than their heads. As they continued, there were a couple of people meditating around the trees. They all stared at the people as they continued walking.

Suddenly, a single bird started chirping. When Isabel looked up at the bird, she yelled out that it was the same kind of bird that was at her window. Anthony looked at it carefully squinting his eyes.

He told them he had never seen a bird like that before. Lucy smiled and told them it was one of its kind and supposedly would never die. The siblings had never heard of that before. Anthony asked what it was called. Cole told them it was a cosmic spirit bird, and Chava told people to listen, and they could hear the messages the bird was trying to tell them.

Angela asked if they could hear the messages. The siblings stared at it when suddenly it disappeared.

Cole told her he couldn't, not yet anyway. Isabel asked if her siblings saw the bird just disappear, and when they said yes, she knew what she saw in the morning.

The bird did not fly away. It simply disappeared. Angela asked how that was possible when suddenly animals walked up around them. The brother and sister told them the animals were there, which means Salman knew they were there. Cole and Lucy began to step back. Rene asked where they were going.

"We brought you here, and now they are coming. Too much energy will overwhelm them. We have to go now," Lucy said as she and Cole walked away.

Isabel knew all too well about energies and yelled out to the brother and sister if that meant the couple were witches.

The brother and sister didn't answer, but they heard a voice, and as they all turned back around, they saw two people with long brown hair. Both were wearing robes. Chava had a band around her head filled with little tiny flowers. The man smiled and told them they weren't witches. They were pure humans.

The animals began to walk away as the man introduced themselves. Angela stared at him with disbelief on her face. Salman looked at her with a smile and held out his hands.

"Daughter," he said.

"It's you, after all these years. I tried finding you but couldn't make it this far. Why are you here, and why didn't you come back?" Angela said without wasting any time.

"My dear, I found the secret, and no one believes me. Here everyone worships me," Salman said. Chava reached out to hug Angela with a huge smile on her face. Angela ran away from them.

The siblings looked at each other. Isabel went to go talk to Angela. Molly asked Salman how he could leave his daughter just to be worshipped. Salman shook his head. He told them he had sent her letters, but they constantly moved, and the birds always kept an eye on her. They were the ones that told him she was coming. Austin asked how the birds could talk to him if he were a human. Salman and Chava looked at each other. Salman explained that witches were once humans, but they were able to form a higher level of consciousness.

The siblings didn't believe that and shook their heads no in confusion. Salman told them he would explain, and they could follow him inside.

Isabel ran up to Angela. She told her to calm down and just hear him out. Angela had tears coming down from her eyes. She told Isabel she and her mother were poor and always moved in with different men all the time. Angela explained that she always wanted to find her father, and when she would cry late at night, the only thing that calmed her down was birds singing at her window, as stupid as that sounded.

Isabel smiled and wiped Angela's tears. She told her it was not stupid, and she had a right to a sincere explanation, apology, and closure because, after all that, she had the ability to start over and move on.

Angela smiled and sat up. She told Isabel that she did deserve all of that, and that's exactly what she would get. Isabel and Angela went back to the others just in time.

Salman said to follow him, and he would explain everything. They followed him into a cabin made of pure wood. When they walked inside, the house was beautiful, and candles were lit all around. Salman walked over to pillows on the ground as there were no couches. He told everyone to sit on the pillows, and he would explain to them what he'd found out and what it all meant.

Salman took a deep breath and looked up slowly as he closed his eyes. The siblings all looked at him, wondering what was about to happen. Chava gave everyone some tea. After a minute of pure silence went by, Salman looked at everyone sitting around him with a smile. He explained what happened to him years ago. He and Angela's mother were hiking up the mountain. When Angela's mother started getting nauseous, she claimed she was feeling motion sickness and dizzy.

The air density changed, and something was off. Angela's mother got upset and told him she couldn't go any higher. She wanted to go back down, but Salman wanted to go higher. He felt like maybe he shouldn't leave her. Angela's mother told him if he wanted to see the top to go ahead. She would
wait for him down below. Angela's mother walked down around the mountain and back into the forest. Salman, on the other hand, just kept climbing. He felt different but not sick.

Instead, it was a good feeling. Suddenly, he felt the

mountain shake just a little, but enough for Salman to stop and look at the ground. He saw two human beings inside the mountain as the mountain opened up to let the humans out. Salman asked them how they got in there. Then suddenly, it closed back up. The two beings stood and stared at him.

They told him they were looking for a hydra. Salman didn't know what that was and told them he had never heard of that before. The two beings walked away without saying another word.

Salman looked at the mountain that was open and closed again, all on its own. When it opened, power poured out and into the wind. He looked back and watched the people walk away from him. Suddenly, Salman heard music coming from the mountain. He placed his ear toward the rocks. He listened to a sound that he had never heard before, and the music was heard throughout his body. From that day on, he was able to listen to the sound of everything.

The siblings looked at each other. Angela asked him even the things that didn't make a sound?

That was when Salman shook his head no and told them that everything made a sound.

He explained that the source of all that was physical in our existence is sound because, with a vibration, there would be a sound. The vibration came off the mountain and into the wind, trees, plants, and everything that had energy. He found out through his research that most humans couldn't hear all the sounds everything was making. All vibrations weren't available to the human ear. Only a small amount of frequency was heard.

The mountain brought the necessary Sadhana to go beyond their limitations of a higher frequency. Isabel told him they did feel stronger, but they didn't think they were in a state of Sadhana. Salman nodded in understanding. He told them they would know if they were. They would not only begin to hear sounds beyond their spectrum, but humans would form a higher level of consciousness and become a natural evolution of a human being—what some might call a witch.

The siblings all looked confused.

Molly said, "What if they were already a witch? Then what?"

Salman looked at them all curious as Chava stood up and asked if they were witches. The siblings did not know what to say. Molly said it was just a question. Salman smiled and told them a witch was just a future human. Everyone felt goosebumps throughout their bodies.

Angela asked him then why there were witches in their universe and, most of all, their world mixed with humans. Salman explained that the first witch carried an ability. In his research, he found that when a human was in a state of Sadhana and experienced higher vibrations, it could evolve an individual into a universal entity.

He continued to say that when the individual become one, it would be engraved inside their blood, which was when the witch inside was born. Chava said that not all humans reached that ability, but every single one of them had access to it.

Anthony asked if he ever saw those beings again, the two from the mountains. Salman shook his head yes, he'd heard of a man with Alzheimer's who died. When he saw a picture in the newspaper, he saw that that gentleman was one of the men.

Salman told them that he didn't think he had Alzheimer's because he was a magical being from the mountain. Isabel asked what it was about the mountain that caused vibrations. Chava answered, thinking they knew already that the mountain was a door to the parallel universe.

"We are looking for the Sun Witch, is that where she is from?" Rene asked.

Salman opened his eyes wide. "How do you know about her?" he asked.

"We just have to find her because she is the one to open the heaven dimension," Rene explained.

Salman and Chava looked at each other. They were so happy that others had heard of the Sun Witch.

"The parallel universe is in the fifth-density and carries more magic than this universe. Two witches held the power without being human. It was their protection and love for the humans that witches were able to thrive throughout the universe because, without a human, there would be no more new witches in the future of both universes," Salman said.

The siblings thanked him for his help but asked one more question. They wanted to find a way to open the mountain. Salman told them they needed to find the being that was still alive unless he found another way to go back, but he would know. That man walking somewhere on their planet came through the wormhole from the parallel universe years ago.

The siblings finished their tea and placed their cups on the wooden table against the wall, making room for the circle of pillows on the floor. Isabel told Angela before they left to search for the man that she should speak to her father. Angela agreed, and the siblings said their goodbyes for now and waited in the front by the garden of vegetables. Chava stayed with them and showed them her garden. Angela stood with her father inside the room of pillows. It was silent for the first five seconds.

"I never walked away completely. I always tried to reach out, but the letters kept coming back. I had to stay here. This is where I belong. I tried to talk to your mother, and even my mother, and everyone just thought I was crazy. When I became enlightened and was able to hear the vibrations, that's when I sent the birds to you," Salman explained.

"The birds. I knew they were trying to tell me something, but I couldn't understand," Angela replied.

Salman walked over to a drawer that held a small wooden box. He opened the box, and she saw pictures of her from all different ages. He then took out a necklace with a rock inside a metal bracket. He put down the wooden box and placed the necklace around her neck. Salman told Angela the rock was part of the mountain, and when the birds told him she was coming, he wanted to give her a piece of the magic.

"I love you, and I am sorry you felt I didn't care. I do and I always will. Wear this necklace and meditate. The necklace will help you get into a state of Sadhana faster than ever before. You are always welcome to stay here," he said.

Angela didn't want to leave her mother alone. Her mother had a hard time taking care of herself, let alone Angela.

"Maybe in the future, but for now, I need to stay and help my mother."

Salman understood and told her that even though his blood was marked as a universal entity after she was born so he couldn't pass the magic onto her, she could become one now and pass it on to her children.

Angela nodded and held her necklace, and at that single moment, her anger toward her father passed through her like a calm breeze by the ocean floor.

They hugged, and Angela met the siblings back outside. As they began to walk away, Isabel asked how it went talking to her father. Angela shrugged her shoulders and told everyone that she would learn from her parent's mistakes and grow from them.

They both tried to find their happiness, but it wasn't with each other. Angela planned to go back, but first, she wanted to make sure her mother found her happiness. Then Angela would begin her journey to find hers. After all, she was graduating high school this year. She knew she had to decide what and where she wanted to be.

As the siblings continued walking, Isabel asked where they should start looking for the man who came out of the mountain. Molly held out her hand to stop them from walking. She told them it wasn't where they should start looking; it was *when*.

She held out her hands and told them maybe they couldn't go back and see Sef with the Sun Witch because it wasn't in this universe. Perhaps they just couldn't travel to the parallel universe, but if the men entered there, they could travel precisely to that moment. They all smiled and held out their hands. Anthony told Angela to wait there because she was a human and might not be able to travel. Angela held onto her necklace and told him she would stay but planned to travel through time in the future.

The siblings knew she wanted to raise her consciousness just like Salman told them because they could open their minds and evolve into a witch.

Not the ones with a pointy hat that you see on TV but the ones who could listen to a single vibration and hear the sound of even the trees. Every living thing tried to communicate with the human beings in this universe and the Earth we lived on. If you could listen to the trees, you would hear them singing and sometimes even hear them pleading to save them. *Save the trees.*

~ 3 ~

THE SUN WITCH

The siblings brought Angela back home to her mother. As she walked inside, she finally understood why Isabel missed school so many times, while the principal and teachers never seemed to question them. She asked if they would be back in time for school on Monday. Isabel smiled and told her they always went back. She would see her in class. Angela laughed and shook her head, thinking that after everything they went through, they always made it to homeroom, if not Monday, then most likely Tuesday. She asked if they were ever afraid something would happen to them. The siblings looked at each other, and Isabel told her not to worry. They would always come back.

Angela smiled telling Molly, Isabel, and Austin she would see them on Tuesday as she walked inside her house. Smiling back at her, the siblings gathered hands and went back in time to the moment the two beings came out from inside the mountain.

They stood a few feet away as they watched Angela's mom walk down the mountain and her father continue to walk higher just as he said. He seemed eager to look at the top of the mountain. Suddenly, they saw him stop and stare as the siblings squinted their eyes and walked a little closer to see what he was looking at.

That's when they saw it. The mountain started shaking, and they could see him stare at the crack that started growing bigger and bigger.

They watched as two men walked out of the mountain, and the opening began to close behind them. When the men were talking to Salman, they saw him. He was a third being that ran out just as the mountain closed, and nobody saw him except the siblings. The two men talked to Salman and the third man they saw run out looked all too familiar.

It was Sef, the third man, running and hiding behind a huge rock.

He stayed there until the two men walked away, and then Sef came out of hiding. He looked at his watch and began to run as far away from the men as possible. The siblings looked at each other as they believed Sef wasn't with the men looking for the creature. Instead, it looked like he wasn't supposed to be in this universe at all.

Anthony told his siblings that if Sef wasn't looking for the creature like the two men were, then that leaves the question of why he snuck out and what he was trying to do.

The siblings agreed to go back to Alair to find the answers because Sef knew something, and they weren't taking no for an answer anymore. They still wanted to see their father and make it to the heaven dimension, but now they knew Sef wasn't from just any universe; he was from the one universe that not only caused death to those who cross over, but after seven days, it would cause a significant change in time and space for them all. The Hydra died because it couldn't continue living in this universe, and his blood was used for potions that were stronger than any other potions a witch had made before. The siblings were determined to find out why he hid from the other men. So before they went back to find that other man, they wanted answers from Sef.

They arrived on Altair right in front of the university. Some of the students stared at all the siblings when they walked inside to the stairs. As they walked lower and lower to the basement, it got darker and darker. When the siblings got to the basement, there was a locked door. The siblings called out for him and knocked on the door. There was no answer. Anthony pulled the lock off, and the door still wouldn't open. Rene told them to stand back; the door was sealed with a spell. They all stood back as Rene said a couple of words and lifted her hands.

Suddenly, the door opened, and Molly was the first to walk in and see the pictures on the wall. There were writings and pictures of the planets and wormholes. The scripts were confusing to the siblings, but as they all continued to read everything on the wall, they saw that Sef had written that each planet had a hidden doorway to the parallel universe. Sef also wrote in red marker with exclamation marks that the parallel universe held the answers he couldn't remember.

The siblings looked at everything on his wall when Sef walked in on them. He screamed how they dare come into his home. The students were not allowed down there. Anthony told him they didn't want it to come to this, and that he was sorry for barging into his home. They needed answers because the university taught them that there were universes the Crescent witches could travel to, but the universe that sat parallel to this one, not even the Crescent Moon Witches could crossover. And yet he was from there.

Now he continues to live in this one. Anthony asked him how that was possible? Sef started laughing, telling the siblings he wasn't from the parallel universe. The siblings looked at each other. Molly told him to stop hiding everything they knew when he came out of the mountain. Sef stared at Molly in confusion.

"How? How do you know about that mountain?" he asked.

"We saw you, Sef. We saw you come out of the mountain," Molly answered.

Sef looked shocked as he walked to the wall. "I'm not trying to hide anything," he said pointing to the papers on the wall. "I really don't remember."

"Then how did Tulin know you met the Sun Witch before?" Austin asked.

"Well, I have dreams sometimes, very intense dreams, and one was me as a child talking to the Sun Witch. I've had that same dream nights at a time. Then, as years went by, I would dream of a mountain I have never seen before, which I've told Tulin in private," he explained. "Tulin would tell me that maybe it really was a conversation with the Sun Witch. It might have been a memory coming out of my dreams. When he told me that, well, I started this wall of information."

The siblings were looking at Sef and everything on the wall. Sef told them that he always thought something happened to him, and he just couldn't remember, but he was trying to.

The siblings all looked at Austin. He told them he was telling the truth. There was no memory before Altair and becoming the building's man at the University of Witchery.

"Oh, my moon power!" Rene yelled.

"What?" Molly asked.

"Well, humans say oh my god, so I say oh my moon power," Rene said as everyone looked confused. "Never mind. It's not important. I know what happened. This is the spell of taking someone's memory."

"Oh, like what you did to me that time," Austin said to Rene as he slightly nudged her.

"No, I've done so many spells to reverse memory loss spell. Nothing worked," Sef explained.

"We are talking about a strong-ass memory spell then," Rene said as she looked at her siblings. "Only the healer's touch can break the spell, am I right?" she asked.

The siblings smiled as they thought Rene was right. They nodded.

"This kind of spell might only be broken with the healers touch," Anthony said looking at Sef.

"When I was under that spell last year, I started to remember again when Isabel kissed my forehead," Austin said.

Isabel smiled. "I didn't know I was the one to break that spell."

Everyone looked at Isabel as she walked slowly toward Sef and held out her hand. Isabel focused on what she was trying to accomplish. It wasn't just a touch of her hand. She used her mind, body, and soul.

His pupils began to grow, and they saw in his eyes something happened. Seconds went by, and Sef pulled away. He remembered everything!

Sef yelled out asking if he had just lost his memory and a healer just helped him with a single touch. Molly wondered why he would ask when it just happened.

"Um, yes, it literally just happened," Molly said. "I mean you were there."

Sef wanted to make sure this was real. Remembering everything, he began ripping all his papers down. He said that he would now die if he weren't back in the other universe in seven days. Sef paced back and forth, explaining that when he first came to this universe after seven days, he would have memory loss of his life in the other universe.

Only a healer's touch could make him remember, and then he could only live seven more days unless he made it back to his universe.

He looked at the calendar and saw he had time to warn them still. He told them he knew why he was here, and it was the moon and Sun Witch who caused the spell to erase the memory because with the memory of crossing over for more than seven days he would die, so forgetting was the only thing to keep him alive.

Anthony asked what happened to the other man because they heard one had died already. He shrugged his shoulders and told the siblings he didn't know what happened to them. He wasn't there to find the Sun Witch's creature as the other men were, but instead, he was there to save three planets from exploding in the year 2023. The siblings looked confused. Sef explained in a panic that the Sun Witch spread apart into two bodies, but their power was not separated in phases of the moon like all of them.

Instead, the two Sun Witches in the parallel universe were the most powerful. Being the most powerful, they couldn't warn the moon witches themselves because the two galaxies would collide and cause destruction that will kill all life in both universes that sit parallel to each other.

Rene asked Sef if that means they couldn't step foot in the parallel universe. Sef nodded told them that was exactly what they couldn't do. The Sun Witch didn't want to die for good, so she kept the secret that three planets and their people would die in the future.

"So why would you come and warn us when the Sun Witch prohibited it? Wouldn't you be afraid of death?" Austin asked.

"I heard the plan to send the two men into this universe, but it was only supposed to last seven days. They were supposed to meet back at the mountain with the Sun Witch's creature, but they couldn't find it, and then they lost their memory," Sef explained. "I took advantage of the opening because death would come to me anyway."

"How?" Isabel asked.

"The planets that carried beings are dying and exploding in my universe. It all started already one by one. I couldn't save my son," he said.

"What happened to your son?" Rene asked.

"My world was one that exploded."

"So where were you?"

Sef looked down to the ground in disappointment. He told the siblings he and the two men worked for a secret organization on planet Earth that searched for other planets that were completely empty ones that wouldn't explode. They found one, but when they were finally able to get there, the Sun Witch told them that the planet was off-limits. Anthony asked if he ever found out why, and Sef told them it was because millions of trees were everywhere.

The siblings looked confused and wondered why that mattered. Sef shook his head and told them not just any trees but particular trees.

The wood from each tree could kill the Sun Witch, and in this universe, could do the same for the moon witches. The siblings were shocked and thought about what Finn had said about the only piece of wood that could kill the Crescent Moon Witches. Isabel told Sef that they believed it might be the wood that turned them evil.

So the one Marcus hid wasn't the only one left. Instead, there was a planet millions and millions of light-years away with trees filled with the only weapon possible to turn the energy the Crescent Moon Witches have inside of them into evil darkness.

Sef explained that if anyone tried to reach the planet, they would turn into something disgusting and unimaginable. Isabel asked what they would turn into exactly. Sef shrugged his shoulders and told them he could never see the other men who came back because the Sun Witch trapped them on the planet to keep an eye on all the trees.

"She warned everyone, and they didn't listen," he said.

Molly told them she couldn't believe it. "So the men who were stuck guarding the trees turned into some sort of creature, and the three planets had already started exploding," she said out loud, trying to process everything.

Sef nodded and told them that he and his man were too late. They couldn't save the planets, and they couldn't save the men on the forbidden planet.

Isabel asked if he was on planet Earth and wasn't hurt, then what planets exploded.

"Gliese, Trappist, and Cassini," Sef said as the siblings held their mouths. "My home planet Cassini where my son and his mother died."

"Cassini is your home planet?" Austin asked as he then read Sef's mind and took a step back.

"What happened, Austin?" Molly asked.

Austin sat on the ground and put his hands on his head. He told Sef to tell everyone his son's name. Sef told them his name was Graham, and he came to this universe to save his son and planet Cassini from exploding because it was coming and the Sun Witch found her pet more essential to find and take back than to simply warn this universe.

Sef told them their universe was further in the future than this one, but only minor things were different.

He overheard the Sun Witch claim the explosion of three planets were just too big of an event not to happen in this universe, but she didn't want to warn them because her life would be in danger when stepping onto this side.

Isabel asked if they were as strong as the Sun Witch then why didn't they know an explosion would be coming. Sef told them the moon witches were strong as each phase of the moon with its own unique power, but together, they would be just as strong as the Sun Witch and would be able to step inside the heaven dimension.

The siblings took in all the information Sef told them and now knew they couldn't step inside the parallel universe but didn't need to.

Instead, they needed to find all the moon witches because they could finally step inside the heaven dimension with complete moon power. Not just one from each phase of the moon like they'd met before for another spell to help save the other side, but this time, all of them if they wanted to see their father again.

Sef told them he traveled to Altair because, in his universe, the Sun Witch was reborn and living on the planet in her recent years. He thought maybe that was where the moon witches would be. But by the time he got there, he'd lost his memory of what he came to do and met Tulin, and the rest was history.

The siblings knew they had to find all the moon witches, but first, Sef told them he had to go back home and for them to find him in that universe to help him save the three planets.

They all agreed as Tulin came downstairs and asked what was going on. Sef held Tulin's shoulder and told him he had been a wonderful friend to him, but the siblings would explain everything. He had to go back home to where he came from, and he told him to find him again in this universe.

Tulin smiled and didn't know what had happened but knew all along Sef's dreams were indeed telling him something that the Crescent Moon Witches had helped him with.

Tulin and Sef hugged as Molly asked how he would get back. Sef told them that when the Earth shifted, the mountain opened. Isabel told him that it happened every thousand years, and it had happened recently already. Sef smiled and told them that he would just go back and that as long as they didn't interfere when he came out of the mountain none of this would change. He just needed a time traveler.

Molly agreed as Sef held onto Molly's shoulder. He smiled at Tulin and nodded his head. He then told the siblings to find him in this universe. They disappeared. Molly took him back to the very moment the Earth shifted as Sef said goodbye and told her to please save his son.

Molly told him she would as he walked back into the mountain but not before his past self walked out.

Austin told them when she returned, they had to find Graham and tell him what they'd learned. One year from now, three planets in their universe would explode, and they had to find a new world to live on and save the species from all three planets that were in danger of dying. They all agreed but also needed a day to rest. They all walked back upstairs and outside to get some fresh air while waiting for Molly to return.

Suddenly, Molly reappeared, and the siblings went back to planet Earth to tell their mother everything because no matter what danger was coming, the siblings always went back to their mother. She would help them on another journey to save their universe.

~ 4 ~

LEFT BEHIND

The following day was Monday; Thanksgiving weekend was over. They all knew everyone was returning to school. Yes, they wanted to find more about the other man who came through the portal, and yes, they wanted open the heaven dimension to see their father. But knowing that in one year, three planets would explode, including Cassini, was on the family's mind too much. Ladle told them to try and find Graham, and she would deal with the school. She felt terrible that her children had to save everyone while they were still children themselves.

Anthony told Ladle that Graham put up a spell to block them from tracking him, so they would need the wolves in New Orleans to sniff out Graham wherever he was. They knew he wanted to stay in New Orleans, so that was where they were hoping to find him.

The siblings teleported to New Orleans once again, and Molly couldn't help but think of Kevin.

They all met up with Amanda and the wolves. Amanda still had the bracelet on, but Danny's spell was strong on her mind, and she continued to obey his orders to help all creatures, including the witches. Anthony asked the wolves to spread out because Graham had to be around this city somewhere. Amanda nodded as all the wolves scattered throughout the town. Everyone was looking around when Austin secretly pulled Amanda to the side.

"I think it's time you tell me why you lied about where you're from," Austin said as he held her arm and pulled her gently behind a tree. "I read your mind, and you knew I was. Why don't you want anyone to know you are from Cassini?"

"There is just a lot of crap in my past I want to forget, and this stupid bracelet is fighting with the sired bond I have with Danny. I can't even think straight," Amanda said as she touched her bracelet which was now part of her skin.

"If I help you get it off, will you trust me to tell me what happened?" Amanda looked at Austin and nodded.

Austin told his siblings he and Amanda would look by the witch's corner. Anthony said okay, but Isabel felt he was lying. She followed them as everyone else looked around near every house, street, and park they could find. Isabel saw Austin go into the witch's store and talk to Bobby. She still believed something was off.

He begged for something. Isabel walked in and asked what was going on. Austin and Amanda rolled their eyes. If anyone was going to follow them, it would be Isabel. Austin told Isabel what was going on even though Amanda disagreed. Bobby explained to them that witches could only go forward in time, so they would need to set up a spell to go back. She told Austin it would take a bit of time because she had to gather the witches.

"Why didn't you just ask Molly.' Isabel asked.

"Why do you think? I don't want everyone to know what was going on," Austin answered.

"Oh, stop. They would help no matter what," Isabel said.

"This being a secret was my idea. Thanks anyway," Amanda said to Austin. "Yeah, you might as well just ask Molly."

They walked a few blocks down to Molly.

"Molly, can you do us a favor and help get this bracelet off of Amanda," Austin asked.

"Um, now? How many things are we doing at once? One thing at a time people," Molly answered. "More important things going on." She started walking away from them.

Amanda wanted to punch Molly in the face, but Danny's spell was potent. She was fighting herself inside her head. Austin knew this. That was why he didn't want help from his siblings—too many questions. Amanda might not open up if everyone knew.

He grabbed Amanda's hand and then held onto Molly's shoulder and told her to please go back to get a lock of hair from Amanda's ancestor who was a human and had the purest heart.

Molly rolled her eyes. "I'm doing this for Austin, not you," Molly said to Amanda. She thought of a particular ancestor they could use for the spell, but she wasn't sure where in time. Suddenly, they started spinning through the wormhole of time.

"What's going on? Why would they leave now? Have they found Graham?" Rene asked, walking up to Isabel.

"Well, no, but for some reason, I feel it's connected," Isabel said as she and Rene watched them disappear.

The planet was Cassini, and right away, Amanda saw her grandmother. She looked younger, but Amanda knew it was her. She ran to her like she was a little girl again. Molly yelled for her to wait, but Amanda didn't care. She kept running. Molly told Austin they would be seen, and Amanda would change something stupid and cause a considerable impact. Austin told Molly he would control Amanda as he walked toward her.

Molly rolled her eyes because she knew Austin wasn't just helping her for the goodness of his heart. She figured something was going on. Molly followed them at a slow walking pace.

Amanda ran up to her grandma, and just as she was about to speak, a woman called her grandma's name, and she began to walk away. Amanda saw her grandma walk toward the woman and then grab a little girl from the woman's arms.

Austin stood next to Amanda and told her to calm down because nothing could be changed in this period of time, but before Austin could finish his sentence, Amanda said that the little girl was her mother. Austin looked at the little girl and asked Amanda, who was a human with the purest heart? Amanda looked at both her mother and grandmother and told Austin they were both humans, but her mother definitely didn't have the purest heart. Amanda said it as a single tear fell from her eye. Austin stood quietly and just looked at the family.

"Okay, listen. We can't change anything. We are here for your grandmother's hair and that's it," Austin said to Amanda as Molly came closer. "We just need to find out how."

Amanda shrugged her shoulders. She ran up to her grandmother and pulled a piece of her hair. Molly held her mouth as that was the fastest and easiest mission ever. Amanda's grandmother looked over and held her head.

"Oh, sorry, my ring got caught in your hair as I waved to my friends," Amanda said.

She pointed to Austin and Molly. The grandmother looked and smiled and said okay in a friendly, polite voice. Amanda knew it would be that easy as her grandmother was the nicest person Amanda had ever known.

As Amanda and Austin grabbed Molly's arm to go back to their time, they heard people scream. The three of them all looked over and started walking toward the screaming, and that was when they saw them. A couple of blocks away from

Amanda's family was Graham's grandmother and his family of witches. Austin and Molly looked at Amanda.

"This planet is huge, and it just so happens Graham's grandmother and your grandmother live blocks away. You knew Graham?" Austin asked.

"I told you to get this bracelet off, and I will tell you," Amanda said.

Molly smiled as she knew something was going on with the two of them. Molly grabbed their hands and told Amanda that not only was she not even from the universe Kevin was in, but she lied about her own home planet, too. Molly laughed and continued to tell Amanda she couldn't wait to hear her reasons.

When the three of them returned, Isabel, Rene, and Anthony were all waiting for them. Austin glanced at Isabel.

"We are all helping to look for Graham, so we all should be aware of what is going on and if it has to do with his father," Isabel said to Austin.

"Yeah, Amanda, why don't you share what is going on?" Molly said.

Amanda looked at Austin, and she didn't have to say a word. He told them they were first going to help her remove the bracelet, and then she would talk. Austin walked toward the witch's corner, and Amanda followed right behind him with the lock of her grandmother's hair.

The rest of them looked at each other and then began to follow. The witches helped with the potion to take the bracelet off Amanda as the rest of the wolves continued searching for Graham. When Amanda was finally free of the bracelet, she gave it to Bobby and told her to keep it. She couldn't be sired to a hybrid and have the power that the bracelet gave of disconnection—no humanity.

Her mind was fighting with herself every day, and Molly knew what that felt like. She put her pride aside and placed her hand on Amanda's shoulder, and for the first time ever, Amanda smiled at Molly. Austin was happy they did that. After all, Molly always had a problem with making friends with other girls. She claimed they were all mean, and boys were easier to be friends with.

The room was silent for a couple of seconds when Austin told Amanda it was time to speak up and asked if she knew anything about Graham or his father. Amanda took a deep breath as she opened the shop's back door and sat on a log. The siblings all joined her and sat around the firepit. Amanda explained what happened and how her parents did, in fact, know Graham's father and why they were killed. As soon as she saw him, that was the real reason she wanted to stay because she was done running.

Rene asked why she was running in the first place.

Amanda explained the story. Isabel and Rene looked at each other. It was all connected.

Years ago, Amanda's parents worked for a secret organization on planet Earth. They were in charge of a mission to find a planet that had no life except water and plants. Everything else they planned on creating.

They searched and searched for years. All through Amanda's childhood, her parents weren't around. They left Amanda with her grandma most of the time, and when they traveled back to Cassini, Amanda always tried to get their attention.

They became obsessed and planned to move only the rich to a better and new planet and were going to leave the poor to fend for themselves. Amanda told them that one day her parents found a man to help with their mission because finally, they believed they had found something. Amanda was very nosey and always tried to listen when her parents whispered or thought she was asleep upstairs.

Amanda heard them say they were going to use him to see if the planet was habitable. That was all Amanda heard, and days went by when suddenly her parents started paying more attention to her and being home a lot more. Amanda thought everything was going to be okay, and maybe their mission was successful. They were home and playing with her—something they never used to do.

Then one day, they told her they all had to move further away. Amanda wanted to pack her clothes and belongings, but she didn't have time for any of that. One night, her father came into her room and carried her to the forest. They sat there while Amanda asked why they were there so late and what was happening.

Suddenly, a woman appeared, who Amanda now knew was Madam Marel.

The siblings looked confused. Austin asked why Graham's mother would help them all leave. Amanda looked down at her fingers, and she took another deep breath as if she had never told anyone this before. She explained that the man they were using for testing the planet was Graham's father. His name is Sef. Madam Marel wanted him gone, so when she found out they needed a test subject on a planet she already knew was off-limits and secured with a spell no witch could break, she used black magic to lure Sef to them. He would never have left his son for anything, and Madam Marel sent him there and told Graham he had left them.

Amanda continued her story. She told them they were sent away because the mission was never successful like she'd thought. Instead, it went horribly wrong, and the test subject, who was someone's father, was turned into a disgusting creature and left behind. The siblings knew what happened because it was almost the same thing as the parallel universe. Instead, Sef was the one who was left behind. Rene asked if he was still there to this day.

Amanda answered, "Most likely because the whole organization was shut down."

Molly asked why they left him behind like that and why they didn't continue their work. Amanda explained that everything would most likely have continued because her parents would have gotten a new test subject. But Sef had a secret girlfriend, and she was a vampire. The vampire did not leave it alone. She wanted revenge.

The siblings all knew that was why vampires killed her parents. Amanda nodded and told them she knew what they were thinking, and yes, that was why the vampires were after her parents because Sef's girlfriend was furious.

Even if she got him back, he was a disgusting, deformed creature now. Everyone working in the organization who left him there to rot was mysteriously dying one by one. Amanda's parents thought Madam Marel could protect them, but she insisted they go, not to save them but to save herself from being exposed. Madam Marel didn't want the vampires to know she was a part of it. So not only did she use black magic to send Amanda and her parents to another universe, but she also sent Sef's girlfriend to get them so no one would ever know about Madam Marel's involvement.

The siblings were upset and disgusted by what everyone did to Sef. Amanda explained that her parents told her everything because they felt like they were still being chased, and they were right. One night, Amanda watched as vampires, including Sef's girlfriend, ripped her parents apart and sucked out all their blood. Amanda was just so angry at the people who killed her parents, but as she grew, she knew in her heart her parents were the ones who did this. Amanda's mind got worse when she found the bracelet. She just wanted revenge on the vampires.

Amanda didn't want to talk about it any longer. She sat up and told them she would continue to search with the wolves for Graham. They all looked at each other as Amanda walked away.

The siblings knew what they had to do. They had to know how to fix this because they were just as powerful as the Sun Witch.

They had to find all the moon witches because, with them, they could finally remember every single memory they'd endured all of their lives, even the moment they were created. They could remember where the planet Sef was sent to. The siblings had come so far in their power, but now they had to retain all they had done because, with that memory, they would absorb the entire moon power and become one with the moon. The siblings knew who they were in their past lives because they had seen them before, but now they would remember their whole story.

~ 5 ~

MOON POWER

The moon and Sun Witches were more than people with powers. Without any intention, their power created life as neutrons, protons, electrons, photons, and the moon and sun power could create and manipulate every particle that made this universe exist. The beginning of their energy started when they two were created.

Fourteen billion years ago, everything was black. There was no color or sound life as you know it didn't exist. Or so everyone thought; there was something. There was a single world, but it was not like any other planet. It was of light, energy, and consciousness. There was no matter, only total energy. These conscious minds were in a peaceful state, and it would have stayed that way if something hadn't collided with it.

There was a ball of white light, not just one, but three. They appeared from somewhere else in a portal of the highest dimension when they collided with the single world. An explosion happened that on planet Earth now called the Big Bang. It made everything spread out and created a universe with everything it needed to come together and make every planet its own unique world. But every world wouldn't be able to prosper and grow without the sun or moon. That also was for a reason.

There was a portal between the moon and the sun, and that portal was where the power was from. But three lights collided with the planet. The sun, the moon, and the star were the energy that came from the higher dimension, and their portals were hidden in plain sight. Not only in the sun or moon but also in a particular star up in the sky that was seen from every planet in the galaxy. The portals took you to the higher dimension; their home, the place where the three balls of lights came from, was called Larslnazm.

It was a place that formed the most powerful energy, and as soon as the three balls of light left Larslnazm, that was when they appeared in the universe that was about to be created—this very one. With a single touch, the energy made all the light, energy, and consciousness in that very world burst into this very universe they were in today.

Every consciousness found a home, and time was created as the sun brightened the day and the moon shined through the night, and the stars made dreams come alive because every human had the ability to harness the magic that each of them carried: the magic of Larslnazm. It was bursting out of the moon, sun, and star. When humans connected with each other, they were more than a human. They became a universal entity known as a witch here on planet Earth. It was the ability to control and manipulate everything around them with a single thought.

When every human reached enlightenment, Larslnazm would shine out of each of its three portals, and all the universe would become the very place the moon witches were from, and then it started all over. You see, Larslnazm was a world of power, and in order to have that, you needed everyone to carry the power inside of them and become enlightened.

As that happened, this universe would come together, and everyone would be able to see everything in the universe using the power of the mind. Everyone would finally know what was out there and become one world, and that world was Larslnazm. The magic in that world would be known as the sun, moon, and star, and it would continue to create more universes with a single explosion and start again. The Moon witches had to remember....
***

The siblings were resting that night when Isabel got a text. It was Angela. She wanted to know if Isabel was okay and if she would see her tomorrow. While she wanted to see her, Isabel knew she had to find the other moon witches. Isabel texted back that she wouldn't be in school this week but would return soon.

A text came back with a sad emoji. Isabel was also upset; she stared at the text messages, disappointed. Then another followed, saying it was okay to return to school when everything was safe, and she couldn't wait for the adventure stories.

Isabel smiled and texted back, *okay*. She put her phone down, and about five minutes later she fell asleep for the night.

As the sun shined in the early morning, Anthony was heard in the hallway, waking everyone up. When they all met downstairs in the kitchen, they saw Rene was already up reading by the bookshelf. She saw everyone staring at her.

"I couldn't sleep. No sleep, no dreams. So I figured I'd look stuff up to help us find them all," Rene said.

"Okay, did you find something?" Anthony asked.

"Well, not really, except there is a book that we were supposed to read. It was the crescent book of rules and guidance," Rene said.

"Isn't that what father gave us?" Austin asked.

Rene shook her head no and walked over, showing them the page she was reading. She explained that there is another book that was made years before the one their father gave them. While their father's book guided them on each of their abilities, there was another that was all about the moon's power and its phases.

Molly seemed annoyed and asked them why was it they remembered things in their other lives, but were clueless in this one. Ladle walked down the stairs and heard Molly's question.

From what James used to say about the moon witches, she told them that all the phases would one day come together and would remember everything. She explained that in all their lives, there was always a moment when that happened. Some were earlier, and some were later in life. Ladle told them she had heard many stories about the crescent moon power, and she looked at all her children and said to them that she believed this time might even be the earliest.

The siblings looked at each other, and for the first time ever, they thought maybe they were becoming more substantial. They will soon realize it was true because humans were becoming enlightened, and that was how it all began. The siblings had breakfast before quickly teleporting to their first destination. They had an idea where one was located because of the spell they had done before when they needed one moon witch from each phase. Their first place was a small village in southwestern China.

The village was called Zengchong Dong Ethnic Village. It had tiny houses bunched together by a mountain and green farmland. The houses were peasant houses with tiled roofs.

Her name was Hui, and she was the witch of the New Moon. She came from a poor family, and her parents were farmers. When the siblings arrived right away, they were stared at by all the villagers. Women with children by a river washing herbs with no shoes on. Men in artificial wood carriages on the country road as horses were pulling the carriages; not a car in sight. Everyone started going toward a tower, and some went inside as they continued to stare at the siblings.

When passing the tower, it read *Drum Tower*. Anthony told them that it was the Zengchong Drum Tower in Congjiang. The Dong people use it for meetings and events that go on in the village. Suddenly, the drum hanging down from the top of the tower began to ring. Someone was up there banging on the drum.

The siblings knew everyone was suspicious of them. Suddenly, the door flew open, and a woman walked out. It was Hui, and she knew who they were because she was one of the witches who helped them with a spell they had done before. Hui bowed and looked around at all her people.

"*Tāmen píngjìng de lái,*" Hui said. She then looked back at the siblings. "My people were just afraid. They come to me when danger is upon our village."

"We understand. We just need all the moon witches that were created from the powerful energy we have inside of us," Rene said.

"Ah, yes, I dreamt about this moment. Except an older man was standing next to all of you," Hui said.

The siblings looked at each other and shook their heads. Molly asked what he looked like. Hui looked like she was thinking hard. She told them he had a light shining out of his head shaped like a crown and another out of his heart. Hui asked if someone they knew had a very old soul and was in the heavenly dimension. The siblings all said yes, wondering how she could see him. Hui said she could see some of the people there, but she couldn't hear or talk to them.

Hui explained to the siblings all the moon witches had different unique powers, but only the Crescent Moon Witches held the power of the empathic healer. The siblings all looked at Isabel.

Hui told them all the phases came from one ball of energy, and it all started with the healer.

When they all came together under the moon, their minds would once again be one. Molly asked how she knew all that. Hui smiled and told them she had something that belonged to them. They followed her inside. Inside were four giant pillars with benches between the pillars. In a circle, the central fire pond stood.

Hui saw them looking at the fire. She told them the fire was on all year round and only shut off if the New Moon witch died. The siblings looked at Hui. She continued to walk and told them that her body would disintegrate when they came together, and her power would have to be reborn into a new body until they met again.

"Wait, what? You're going to die if we do this?" Isabel asked as all her siblings were in shock.

"Yes, the fire will go out until I am back, and then the villagers will know when I am reborn because the fire will then light up again," Hui said as she stopped and placed her hand on a statue.

"We don't want to kill you. Is there another way?" Austin asked.

"This is what has been happening for billions of years. It's what has to happen. It's here in the book," Hui said as the statue began to move and the wall opened up. A single book was held on a gold stand.

"The book of the moon witches. It's for us all, and here is the spell we must do," Hui said as she held the book in her hand and passed it to Isabel.

The siblings all looked over Isabel's shoulder. They read the part where it stated the bodies of the new moon would disintegrate and turn to dust. All the witches would then remember why they were there and all of their lives. When Isabel turned the page, they saw what else it stated. The moon book told them they would also remember where their energy came from. The siblings were in shock. Hui held onto the statue again, and the wall opened even more. They all looked up to see hundreds of golden urns lined up. Hui told them it was okay; this was what had to happen. She would always come back. She then smiled as the siblings still felt horrible and began to think of changing their minds.

Hui told them if they didn't do this, all the enlightened people would forget everything, and witches would disappear into existence. Hui told them she didn't remember everything either, but she knew that this had to be done in every life they had. The siblings all looked again at the urns and at the book. Rene told them that this was the book she had read about, and she took it from Isabel and flipped through it.

She came to the page where it stated a Cresent Moon Witch should not carry a child. The siblings remembered about Mila and Nathaniel when Rene read that out loud. Anthony nodded. He told his siblings this book must have been in all of their lives, which meant they had done this before. The siblings all looked back at the urns. Molly said they definitely had as she looked at the ashes of hundreds of Hui's bodies.

What was left of her flesh and bones and the life she carried for each, was in every one of those urns.

Hui told them it had to be done. The siblings thought maybe they could wait, but Hui said that if they were here now, it was for a reason, and this was the time in this life that they had to do the spell and remember everything. The siblings felt so bad, but three planets would explode in one year, and all its people would die. The siblings had to know where they came from and what they had to do to save the planets and Graham's father from the forbidden one.

Once they remember everything, they would know where this planet was, and they would know everything the Sun Witch was hiding.

Altair might be their family's home planet, but the siblings were more than witches. They came from a higher frequency and a much more powerful dimension. One that resembled this one but was more powerful because this one was the beginning of what would become Larslnazm, the very place they were actually from.

Their minds had to keep up to understand what was happening and why they were here. Listen closely, and soon they would understand. They had to listen to what this planet was telling us because they had to become witches to become Larslnazm once again.

The siblings knew what they had to do. It seemed harsh to take control of Hui's power and mind as her body disintegrated, but that had to be done in every life for the siblings to remember everything.

Austin asked before Hui closed the hidden door, "Why do we forget every time we're reborn?"

Hui wasn't sure how to answer that because it was like that for centuries. She closed the door and told the siblings that she dreamed of the moment Hecate spread all the gods throughout the universe, and even though their energy still lay inside planet Earth, they could live in human form on other planets as the universe grew.

One of the gods was sent to Venus, and she separated herself just like the siblings did long ago.
Her name was Empusa, and now she had three bodies, and they were the natural creation of the gibbous moon power. Hui told them they had to come for the spell as they had to die as well.

Hui explained those witches would know the answer to that question. She told them that the three gibbous witches were here on planet Earth. They didn't know why, but they felt they had to save the humans on this planet years ago.

Hui felt a connection with a small city in the Netherlands, and one day, she met one of them in her dreams. Hui pointed to a map on the table.

"That is where we go next to find them," Hui said.

The siblings all agreed. They were going to meet the three moon witches who were once the goddess known as Empusa.

They all walked in the back of the building holding hands as they needed all the moon witches to remember why they were here, and with the complete moon power, they would have the ability, as the Sun Witch from the parallel universe did, to step inside the heaven dimension and to know everything the Sun Witch remembered about the hidden planet and the explosions.

The moon witches knew all too well from their other lives on a planet made with millions of magical trees that could create magic everywhere but also made from the same wood that could create darkness and evil in a moon witch. Something was causing them to forget in every life, but now they knew they just needed to all come together again.

They closed their eyes, and Hui said out loud they were headed to Oudewater, Netherlands.

~ 6 ~

WICCA

They all arrived in Oudewater, Netherlands. Hui brought them to the first witch they had already met. He had helped the siblings before. His name was Lucas, and he, like his siblings, came from a goddess known as Empusa. She was sent to Venus centuries ago, but now they were all found on Earth with a strong urge to save the humans. The siblings arrived at a building that was now a museum, but hundreds of years ago, it was known for its refusal to sentence witches to death.

When one person was accused of witchcraft, they were weighed because they figured if a witch could fly on a broom, they must not weigh much at all. The Weighhouse in Oudewater didn't want anything to do with sentencing witches.

Now, it was not only a museum but the home of Lucas, who felt safe here since the time he was scaled and wasn't found to be too light. Lucas was not sentenced all those years ago even though he was, in fact, a witch. Lucas had the ability to go in complete meditation and remembered all his lives and every memory except the moment he was Empusa, and that was why he needed the spell of all the moon power.

The siblings and Hui walked into the back of the building and knocked on the door. Lucas answered quickly and welcomed them inside. He was very fidgety and happy to see the siblings and Hui. He told Hui he was delighted to see her and not just in their dreams. He winked at Hui as the siblings smiled and looked at each other. Lucas walked over to each of the siblings and clapped his hands with excitement.

"You are younger than all the other times. This is marvelous!" Lucas said, looking at all of their faces inches away from each of them. He walked around as if he was staring at every pore on their faces. "This is wonderful. The younger you are when it's time to do the spell means the universe is becoming our home!" he said, jumping up and down.

"You have a lot of energy, my god," Molly said as Austin laughed.

"What do you mean by all this? Do you know why we have to do this every time we are reborn?" Anthony said as he stepped back from Lucas, standing too close to his face. "Why does it matter if we are younger when doing this?"

"So many questions. Last time, it was the healer who had all the questions," Lucas said as he poked Isabel's nose.

Isabel started laughing as everyone else joined in. He told them as he backed away and walked over to his window. He placed his hands in his pockets and leaned on a desk. He then explained that the more the universe was filled with witches, the younger they would be when doing the spell. Austin asked what would happen if they came together with all the moon witches as children. Lucas stood up straight, took his hands out of his pockets, and began hugging everyone in excitement. He told them that if they came to him at age thirteen, that was the number when there would be no more humans left; every human would be a witch with a higher consciousness.

Then, they would be home again. Lucas remembered a lot, but he couldn't remember Larslnazm and when or how it happened. He just knew that this universe had to be enlightened to be home again.

Isabel told Lucas about the potion their mother gave them when they were younger, and they didn't have a chance to remember they even had powers. Lucas looked shocked. He told them that had never happened before. He began looking through his books, and when he found the page, he looked up at everyone. He asked them why she did that to them. Rene explained about her hiding on planet Earth and wanting a normal life for them.

Lucas continued to look shocked as he asked if she was trying to make them human. The siblings all looked at each other confused, as Molly said yeah and asked why that mattered. Lucas held up the book and asked them if that was what their mother was hiding from.

The moment they all looked at the book, they saw a picture of Abigor. Anthony grabbed the book from Lucas and stared at the evil he remembered stabbing with his sword. Anthony asked why he was asking this. Lucas told him to read it out loud, and when Anthony began reading right away, it said Abigor was the creation of the Sun Witch. The siblings all grabbed the book one by one. Lucas told them that Abigor messed with time, but that was not all he did. His blood could turn the moon witches back to humans, and they would have no memory of anything ever again—not even when reborn.

Witches would become extinct, and the parallel universe would then wipe out their universe completely because, without magic, this universe would not be able to become Larslnazm. It would stop expanding and begin to get smaller and smaller as something became nothing.

Rene told Lucas their mother wouldn't do that to them. Lucas shook his head and told them that it must have been planned, and he was not saying she did it on purpose, but maybe it played out exactly how the Sun Witch wanted it to. He paced back and forth and held his chin. He said that there was no cure when they drank his blood. At least, he didn't know of one. He then stopped and looked at the siblings.

"How did you remember again?" Lucas asked.

"I never took it," Rene answered. Everyone looked at Rene. "I told them who they were, and they remembered."

"Ah, it makes sense," Lucas said, clapping. "Lucky, lucky, lucky."

"Being you didn't take it, you were the only one we know of to save them," Hui said.

Lucas hugged Rene.

"We were told it would wear off on our eighteenth birthday. That's the only reason my father gave it to my mother in the first place," Anthony said.

Hui and Lucas glanced at each other. "That's not what the book says about his blood. If you all took the potion, including Rene, it might not have happened as you all thought," Hui said.

"Well, I'm glad we don't have to find out!" Lucas shouted, clapping his hands in excitement.

"Why would the Sun Witch send Abigor to us and try to erase our memory for good?" Anthony asked.

Lucas took his book back from Hui's hands and placed it back on his shelf. He told them that he had heard she was greedy but not so evil to try and erase this universe.

He wasn't sure why she would do that. Austin heard Lucas's mind as he was thinking. He quickly told him they knew about her other creation, the Hydra. Lucas looked at Austin with his eyes wide open. He told them that that creation was not supposed to come here. Hui remembered seeing the Hydra in her dreams. She told them that the animal was supposed to keep the humans safe, but when it crossed over, it couldn't survive. Lucas nodded and told them that the Sun Witch created all different creatures to give her what she wanted.

Lucas explained the hydra was to keep her universe safe, but Abigor was sent after the moon witches. The siblings understood what had happened but weren't sure why. Austin asked what everyone else was thinking, what happened to the hydra, and how it crossed over without the Sun Witch knowing until it was too late. Lucas shrugged his shoulders and told them his sister might know.

She was the second body formed from the goddess and the other gibbous witch. He held out his hand toward the door and told everyone she held the hydra's blood. She would know more about the creature.

The siblings were shocked that the same blood that Blair from the other universe had given them, to make one wish, was here, and someone else had it and knew exactly what it was. The siblings followed Hui out the door with Lucas right behind them; they were on to the next moon witch.

Her name is Tessa, and she lived by a beautiful river. Flowers and plants were all around her with a tiny little canoe tied up in the water in front of the home. Across the river, they saw a huge weeping willow tree, just like Blair's home. Before they all reached the door, a lady came out with a black blouse and white pants. She wore her brown hair in a tight bun. Lucas told everyone there was his sister as he pointed and then waved. She smiled, walking toward them.

Tessa introduced herself and told Lucas he was right when he told her this time was different as she held a piece of Isabel's long red hair and told them they looked so young. Lucas introduced everyone to Tessa, and she smiled, hearing their names.

"We came back to this planet just as we too were goddesses, but just like you, we carried the moon power inside of us and made our way back to this planet. We all come from two goddesses that carried the most powerful energy," Tessa said as she smiled and held on to Isabel and Rene's hands. "And you, you are the only one who didn't spread out into different souls," Tessa said as she began to walk toward Hui.

Hui smiled and closed her eyes as Tessa took a step back, wondering what she would do. Seconds later, Hui became hundreds of bodies, and all were identical. They all spoke at the same time and told them her ability was to separate into multiples. The siblings jumped as they weren't expecting that. Hui told them that everyone had a doppelgänger in
every universe, but Hui lived with all of hers inside.

Yet out of all the doppelgängers, she was the only one with moon power. Tessa nodded and smiled as Hui's others became one again.

"Ah, impressive, so when you fight, you will always have an army," Tessa said.

Everyone smiled.

"You are the new moon witch, and without you here, there would be no others," Tessa said, hugging Hui. "One of a kind, no matter how many there are of you. Your eyes are the difference in all of those doppelgängers, and the eyes tell a lot about a person." She turned around and smiled with her hands up. "Also, the healer is one of a kind because none of the witches carry the power of the empathic healer other than the crescent moon power. Without a healer to save us, the new moon wouldn't have a chance to survive. Understand?" Tessa asked as she walked up to Isabel. "We need her, but she needs you."

"Woah, crazy, I'm not high enough for this deep conversation," Molly said.

"Ah. and the traveler. Just like my other sibling, Yara, she is the one who might be difficult," Tessa said as she walked toward Molly.

Right away, Anthony asked about the blood of the hydra. Tessa told them it appeared in her garden one day, and when she did a spell to see what it was, a creature appeared in her mind. Tessa told them something gave her the potion. That something was trying to tell her something, but she didn't know what.

She used the potion one day during a ritual, and
the Earth began to shift. The siblings all looked at each other, confused and shocked. They couldn't believe that might have been the cause of the shift, but they all thought to themselves that if that was true, then something was trying to open the portals and help create enlightenment through the vibration that came out of the mountain.

Suddenly, about twelve people started walking toward them. Lucas asked Tessa who they were. Tessa smiled and asked everyone if they had ever heard of Wicca. She raised her hands as everyone bowed to Tessa. She yelled out to go to the tree, and she would meet them there. Hui asked who they were. Tessa said, smiling, that she had created a way to enlighten humans with her very own religion that she named Wicca.

She told them they didn't know why they came to this planet but knew it had to do with humans and magic, but as years went by and Lucas remembered their past lives, she knew she had to do her part in creating witches. Everyone looked at the people walking toward the trees and sitting down in a circle.

Tessa explained how it all seemed right, and soon, they would remember where they came from and why they were here. Little by little, they found out information about the moon's power, but with the complete moon witches, they would remember before the Big Bang and before the creation of all time and space in this very universe.

Molly asked about the hydra but quickly got interrupted when the sky turned dark for a brief moment and then lit up once again. Everyone looked up and wondered what had happened. Tessa smiled and looked at the group of people holding hands with their eyes closed.

"Follow me first. Meet the humans who are turning into witches right before our eyes," Tessa said. She walked toward the people as everyone else followed. "Come on, let's hurry and see how fast I created them. They can manipulate the clouds," she said, yelling back at the siblings.

They all looked at each other as they followed behind Lucas and Tessa.

"Wow, so it happened so fast? Like, doesn't this magic thing take a while to master?" Isabel asked, walking quickly behind them.

"By creating rituals on special holidays that circle around phases of the moon; solar equinoxes and solstices; elements like fire, water, earth, and air; and initiation ceremonies seemed more productive in our mission than celebrating an Easter bunny," Tessa pointed out. "No offense to the big bunny. I'm just saying, what's the point in that?" Lucas and Austin started laughing.

Tessa sat down with all the people and told the siblings and Hui to do the same. Everyone joined in as the sun was shining, and the weeping willow trees all around were blowing gently in the smooth breeze passing by. Tessa took a deep breath to take in the earth and blow out nothing but positive energy, love, and beauty passed to her people. She explained to the siblings that she once knew a man long ago in another life of hers who was on the right path. He made a religion based on witchcraft.

He was the one who came up with the name Wicca, which means "wise people." Tessa followed his words and knew when he passed. This was exactly what she needed to continue. She told them that she did change a couple of things for it to be accurate, but compared to all the other beliefs, this one would bring humans closer to the earth and moon.

Austin asked about Buddhism because he'd heard that it would help with getting into the state of Sadhana. Tessa smiled and talked about religion. She told everyone in the circle that every human wanted answers as to why they were here and what created them. Tessa talked about a religion that was perfect for humanity, but it didn't satisfy their questions.

Humans needed a physical being, and it had to be in human form. The universe was so much more than that, but they didn't have the higher minds just yet. They were limited to what they saw and heard. The religion known as Taoism believed humans and animals should live in balance with the universe.

Taoists believed in spiritual immortality, where the spirit of the body joined the universe directly after death.

Molly asked, "Isn't that what happened before the other side was created?"

Tessa smiled and nodded but asked who created those people. Tessa told them they believed with the assistance of four creatures, a tortoise, a phoenix, a dragon, and a unicorn.

The Earth was made from a man named Pan Ku. He died; his body was transformed. His left eye became the sun, and his right eye became the moon. His blood became the rivers and oceans, his breath became the wind, his sweat became the rain, and his voice became the thunder. His flesh became the soil, and the human race sprang into being from the fleas living on his body.

Everyone looked at each other as Tessa talked about Buddhism. Buddhists believed that human life was one of suffering and that meditation, spiritual and physical labor, and good behavior are the ways to achieve enlightenment.

Austin said, "Yes, that's precisely right."

Then Tessa smiled and continued about the creation aspect. As Buddha described it, the world began when the Earth and stars spontaneously formed on their own. Water and air then collected and became seas on the Earth. He never continued his explanation about humans and animals, and that was what a lot of humans couldn't settle with. They wanted to know more.

"Yeah but, Pan Ku? You know that isn't how it all formed right?" Molly said.

"My dear, it is just an example of the power we have in everything we are made up of. Our tears, hair, our heart, sweat, and even a single breathe means something," Tessa explained.

Tessa continued to explain that Wicca was enough because once connected to the elements and the moon, the rest would follow into place as long as they followed the rituals she had put into place.

"As long as they become enlightened, they will hear the answers the universe is telling them," Lucas said. "All we have to do is give a simple nudge in the direction of magic."

Tessa nodded.

Isabel said she knew God wasn't a human, but all the kids in her school thought that. Tessa smiled and shook her head. She explained that the word God was more than a human. It was the energy that was made.

Tessa knew there was a big bang but couldn't remember before that and why. She told everyone that no matter the religion, they all believed in some sort of magical phenomenon, whether it was a magical tree with a talking snake or rising from the dead.

There was always a bit of magic in all the beliefs, and that is for a reason. Where there was magic, there would be enlightenment. Molly asked about the ones who didn't believe in anything —atheists. That was what most of her friends from school were.

Everyone looked at Tessa.

"Ah, you see, those people want to be proven wrong. They are constantly asking to be proven wrong. They are the ones who must see to believe. Smart, I'd say. They just want proof, and boy, do they ask for just that," Tessa said. "The problem with that is sometimes the human eye can't see what's really in front of them, so feeling it is sometimes stronger. Your eyes aren't able to see a higher power. That's why when you use your mind and meditate, you will then begin to feel what is there instead of seeing. Once they achieve this practice and reach a state of Sadhana, then they will begin to feel and hear the vibrations before they see anything."

"Yeah, my friends aren't going to meditate," Molly pointed out.

The siblings all understood what she was saying. Isabel smiled and told everyone it was like air. As long as they could feel it, they knew it was there because it wasn't something they could see.

Tessa smiled as everyone took a deep breath, feeling the cool air being sucked into their mouths as they felt it through their front teeth.

"Okay, my people of the moon, I will return in another body. Carry out what I have taught you and please pass it on. When I return I will know more to teach you," Tessa said.

Everyone bowed their head down as Tessa began to get up.

"The more humans that turn into a universal entity, the more powerful energy will be created into each soul. Their blood will then be marked for eternity. That is when the feeling will be strong enough to help those people that have no faith and finally prove them wrong. We must go and find my sister now. She might put up a little fight before she agrees to do this spell," Tessa said as everyone else got up after her.

"Why is that?" Rene asked.

"Well, she had a child in this life, and it will complicate things a little because this body will have to go," Lucas said.

The siblings felt more horrible than before as now a child would be alone without his mother. Tessa began to walk away from her coven as the siblings, Lucas, and Hui followed. She told them that she wasn't supposed to carry a child because this was what had to happen, as stated in the book.

Tessa told them that the boy was named Zayne, and he was the only one who had the ability to connect with the Sun Witch and the Star Witch.

The siblings looked confused as Austin asked who the Star Witch was. Tessa looked at Lucas and told them she didn't exactly know, but the boy had mentioned the name numerous times. Their sister wasn't sure who exactly the Star Witch was, but Zayne told his mother that the Star Witch was parallel to the sun and moon.

"My nephew can communicate with the sun and Star Witch, so maybe he knows something about the hydra coming over to our world," Tessa told them as they held hands.

She thought he was the one who gave her the blood to do the ritual, but she wouldn't say anything until she asked him herself.

~ 7 ~

PARALLEL UNIVERSE

They arrived in a small Municipality in Belgium called Tielt. A tiny little house connected to many beautiful stores and statues everywhere. Right outside her home was a statue of what looked like an angel looking up to the sky. Everyone was looking at the statue when suddenly they heard a calm, soothing voice that sounded like an angel.

"That brings horrible memories, but the townspeople see it as a remembrance of an innocent girl. To them, she is an angel now," the voice said.

Everyone turned around and saw a woman with wavy brown hair dressed in a long white dress with silver and green flowers. She wore oversized sunglasses hiding her big, beautiful green eyes. Her sandals had flowers attached to them, and her toes were painted silver and white. Her hair was wild, but it fit her face so well. She looked beautiful and didn't need makeup. It was a natural tan beauty.

"Yara, you look like a princess as always," Tessa said. "Oh, princess, I am not," Yara said, smiling.

She took her sunglasses and moved them to the top of her head. Yara looked at everyone around her and told them that they were too early and that she was sorry they wasted their time. Just as Tessa was going to speak, they heard another little voice.

Zayne ran over and called out to his mother. His voice was sweet and innocent. Yara hugged her son and quickly put her sunglasses on his tiny little head. Yara told them that she was not ready to leave. She didn't care about what had to be done.

They couldn't see the boy's eyes, and they thought it was strange to put the sunglasses on him. They couldn't see his eyes, but Austin knew he was looking at him. Yara looked at Austin and then grabbed her son and told everyone she was not ready.

She walked into her home, holding her son's arm to follow her inside. When the door slammed shut, everyone looked at Tessa and Lucas. Lucas said they knew she would say that, but he felt like something else was happening. Tessa agreed and explained to the siblings that Yara had always been distant from them ever since they'd arrived on Earth. Molly asked why that was, and Lucas told them that she was a traveler. They felt like one day she traveled, and after she returned, she seemed different. Tessa nodded in agreement and told them it seemed she was searching for something but never told them what it was.

Austin shared with everyone that their minds were closed, and he couldn't get inside.

"Well then, they are hiding something, and we need to figure out what it is," Anthony said.

"Of course we do," Molly mumbled.

"Is the statue of the angel Yara?" Isabel asked.

Tessa and everyone else stared at the statue once again as Tessa told them that Yara had been cursed in every life because of her soulmate's mother.

She has been tortured and beaten in many lives but always looks like a happy princess. Lucas told them that she hadn't been cursed since Zayne was born, and they believed it might have to do with Zayne because she carried a child and hadn't been cursed since.

The siblings looked at each other.

"So maybe Zayne lifted the curse?" Molly asked.

Everyone was thinking, not sure what to say.

"Well, we need to figure out how to change Yara's mind. I understand the reasons she wouldn't want to do this, but we have to. She knows that," Hui said.

"Yes, I know. We might have to spend the night on this one," Tessa said.

Everyone agreed.

That night everyone rested in a small bed and breakfast with only two rooms. Isabel couldn't sleep and walked outside for some fresh air.

She saw the light coming from a shop. She didn't think anything of it until it began to flicker. Isabel looked around to see if anyone else was looking at the window. She saw no one around. The street was dark and empty. Isabel walked a little closer to see what was happening. That was when she saw her. Yara was sitting in a circle of stones. Isabel knew she was doing a spell. She went straight to the window and looked at everything.

When she looked directly in the window, she saw Zayne floating above Yara, sleeping peacefully. Isabel put her hands on her mouth in shock but wondered what Yara was doing. Suddenly, Zayne fell into Yara's arms, and Yara looked directly at Isabel. Isabel didn't know what to do, so she ran back toward the bed and breakfast.

Reaching the door, she glanced back at the window when she saw the room light shut off. She went inside the bed and breakfast trying to process what exactly just happened.

The following morning, everyone woke up to Rene screaming. Everyone ran to her, but Tessa quickly yelled out not to wake her up. The siblings always woke her up to make sure she was okay, but for the first time, they knew she was using her ability and might need her dreams for answers. Tessa told them when everyone was standing around her bed that she was not ready to wake up and to wait until she woke herself up. Rene tossed and turned and screamed, seemingly possessed.

Lucas told Austin to go inside and see what was happening in her mind. Austin looked at Rene and began to go inside her dream. He heard Rene screaming fire and telling everyone to run. A man yelled out that a boy was causing the fire, and then he heard Yara scream to let him go. She pleaded to take her instead. Rene was holding Yara back and telling the men he was just a boy to let him go. Austin reached out to Rene In her dream.

She yelled back to Austin, saying that Zayne would be taken away because he would start a fire. Austin then heard Yara screaming it wasn't his fault. He took the curse from her when he was born.

"*Save my son,*" she shouted. Everyone was looking at Austin when he snapped out of it and told everyone Rene was trying to help Yara. Lucas asked why in a panic. Austin told them that Zayne was cursed and he would start a fire. When he did, the townspeople would take him away from Yara. Everyone looked at Rene. She was breathing heavily and sweating profusely. Anthony told his siblings to stay with Rene and to let him know if Rene said anything else. The rest of them would find Yara before this happened.

"Oh no, I am going with you. Molly and Austin stay here. I saw her last night doing a spell," Isabel said.

"Was it with Zayne?" Tessa asked.

"Yes, why?" Isabel questioned.

"Was he floating on the top of her?" Tessa asked again.

"Yes, why?" Isabel replied.

Anthony had heard about the spell in the university before, so before Tessa could respond, Anthony asked if that meant she was taking the curse from him.

Tessa answered, "Yes, that's precisely what she was trying to do."

They ran as Molly and Austin stayed with Rene. As soon as they came to Yara's door, they heard someone scream behind them. Everyone ran toward the screaming. When they went to the market square, they saw a couple staring at the child. Yara ran toward her boy and told him to keep his glasses on. She ran and put the boy's sunglasses
back on him.

"Wait a minute. Why does he need those big-ass sunglasses all the time? I never realized he always has those on," Lucas pointed out.

"You're right. I always thought it was cute, but there's more to that. Something is very wrong," Tessa said.

Yara was too late. The couple started walking backward, and within seconds, they became fire. Everyone ran toward Yara when she grabbed her son away from the flames. A man started screaming that it was the boy. Everyone knew this was Rene's dream, and it was happening now. Tessa looked at her sister and said she needed to tell them what was going on—now!

She looked scared and nervous as the fire was getting bigger. Then suddenly, Rene, Molly, and Austin ran toward them. Rene yelled at Yara to go back and save all the people because of the fires. She insisted Yara knew what she was talking about.

Yara was about to scream no. She couldn't until she saw it. Molly was holding a necklace that Yara had been trying to get for years. Yara ran and grabbed the necklace. She disappeared, and when she reappeared, everything went back to normal in a matter of a second.

"What just happened? We know something is going on with you, and you can't face this alone, Yara. Tell us what is going on. We know it has to do with the curse that evil lady put on you that's now on my nephew. What are you hiding, Yara?" Tessa said as she held Yara's shoulder. "It's not over, is it?"

Yara looked at her son and fell to the ground. She had tried so hard to lift this curse, but it had dragged her down for centuries. She started crying as Zayne ran to her and hugged her tightly.

"Mommy, don't cry," Zayne pleaded.

"You tried helping me. In every life and nothing is working," Yara cried to Tessa.

Yara looked up, wiping the tears from her eyes. She looked at all the siblings and told them she was sorry about Abigor. She told her son to contact the Sun Witch to help her slow down this very moment. She wasn't ready to do the moon spell. Everyone held their mouths in disbelief. Molly asked what did she do? Yara snapped her fingers, and everyone ended up inside her house.

She explained that she thought it was just the blood of a creature that they had to drink. Yara didn't know what that creature was. She didn't know he was alive and trying to conquer the universe, and when she found out, she had her son contact the Sun Witch again. When she refused to take back her creature, they asked the Star Witch, and she opened the doors so the hydra could defeat Abigor.

"Oh man, so it was you who contacted the Sun Witch to give us the potion. To slow down this very moment, not realizing it could have erased our memories for good if Rene took it?" Molly said in an angry voice.

"Crap, and she was the one who asked for the hydra to come to our universe and defeat Abigor after realizing he was destroying everything," Austin said.

"Yeah, well, it didn't happen as you planned. I had to kill Abigor. We had to clean up that mess," Anthony said.

"I know, and I'm sorry. It was my mistake to contact the Sun Witch. But don't blame the Star Witch. She was just trying to help. We didn't know that the hydra couldn't last in this universe," Yara said.

"So if her creatures couldn't last here then how did Abigor?" Molly asked.

Yara held the necklace up. "This very stone," she said.

It was from the parallel universe, and it was the only thing that could keep someone or something alive in a parallel universe. Yara asked Molly how she found it. Molly told them that Rene screamed for Molly to go back and find the necklace.

"Yara, you told me in my dream that you've been searching for this necklace. But you've been banished from ever finding it," Rene explained.

Yara started crying again as Zayne hugged his mother's leg tight.

"That's true. The love of my life is the son of an evil woman," Yara explained. "She put my traveling ability inside the necklace and hid it in the past where I couldn't go."

"So why didn't you ever ask for help? Yes, us, but more importantly, your sister and brother?" Isabel asked.

"This curse she placed and taking my ability away was more potent than anything I have seen before. Yes, I could have asked for help, but the thing is, once this necklace returns to my hand, the evil witch will rise again. And well, I didn't want to put that on anyone. I wanted to find another way," Yara explained.

"Oh great, so now an evil witch is on her way? Why the hell did you tell me to get that necklace?" Molly asked Rene.

Rene felt guilty, but she told everyone that Yara told her to in her dream. Yara held the necklace and told them that Zayne was never supposed to carry the curse.

"It's fine. I'm going back to stop this curse before Zayne was ever born," Yara said.

"Yeah but changing something so drastic... What if something goes wrong with this present?" Lucas asked.

"I'm erasing this curse then, and only then will I do the moon spell and let go of this body," Yara said, very determined and confident.

Suddenly, the floor began to shake, and black smoke was seen in the sky. Molly yelled out she was traveling and to grab on.

Everyone did and disappeared, but the second Yara was about to travel, the necklace broke off, and she was left behind. The power to travel was inside the necklace. Yara quickly tried to hold the stone and travel as it flew from her hands across the room.

Everyone was gone except for Yara.

"You found the necklace, did you? With the help of the Crescent Moon Witches," the voice screamed as the floor shook faster and faster.

Yara was furious. Not only had this confrontation lasted for centuries, but now her son was sent in time without her. She couldn't use her ability to travel. She screamed out as loud as she could. She knew she had to fight back alone once again, but this time, the others were in the past, hopefully saving her from this very moment.

The rest of them were in the year Yara was cursed. The year 1579 when the first fire happened.

"Where's Yara?" Lucas asked.

"Mommy?" Zayne cried.

Everyone looked around. Rene told them she thought her power was back with the necklace. Tessa held her head nervously. She said something must have happened, and maybe the evil witch was back.

Isabel held Zayne's hand and told them they had to find the wicked witch and stop the curse. Molly asked if it would change important events if they did this. Tessa and Lucas looked at each other.

"Maybe not. We are not sure, but black magic never has a spot on someone's timeline. Meaning this curse might not have been something that was supposed to happen. We might actually be changing back to what should have been," Tessa explained.

Every torture and whipping that happened to Yara wasn't the life of a moon witch. That wasn't something they were supposed to endure.

She told them that only one person and his followers could cause such a curse upon a moon witch. Everyone looked at Tessa when she told them they were called Satanists and that they carried dark energy inside them.

The siblings all looked at each other because they knew all about dark energy.

"How did they get that dark energy inside of them?" Anthony asked

"His name is Damion. It started when he found a magical tree and turned a powerful witch into darkness. The goddess Hecate was devastated and sent the darkness away," Tessa explained.

The siblings had heard this before and asked if Damion had a child. Tessa shook her head yes and looked at Lucas.

"Lucas was the one who remembers that," Tessa said.

Everyone looked at Lucas.

Nodding, he said that Damion's son went by the name Marcus, and he turned into a vampire years ago. He holds the weapon to the magical tree his father Damion gave him to send the other moon witches away.

"The other moon witches?" Rene asked.

"Well, the lunar eclipse moon power was the one that was sent away. It was in a body that only could access power through an eclipse. He stayed close to you all until he was turned to darkness," Lucas explained.

"We heard he was Hecate's companion. Damion sent him away?" Rene asked.

Tessa said yes. as she began to walk, she told them that Damion did a ritual with the stick from the magic tree, and the darkness went through hundreds of people's noses and mouths, and they became his followers. One of them was Yara's soulmate's mother. Molly grabbed Tessa's arm to stop walking and asked her why they were there.

"Are we stopping the evil, wicked witch who made the curse or Damion?" Molly asked.

"No, we can't control what Damion has done. Hecate already tried. That was a fixed point in time. The magic of the tree cannot be undone," Tessa said.

"Every magic can be undone," Rene said.

Everyone looked at Tessa as they thought the same thing.

"For now, we just stop the curse from happening," Tessa said as she continued to walk.

Molly followed and told her they would, but that was not all they would do because if Damion was stopped, then her friend Danny would be saved from being a hybrid.

"Maybe with all of us, we could reverse the magical tree's power and darkness, but Marcus will still become a vampire because your friend's father chose the power of the vampire and sacrificed his father to become one," Tessa said, turning around to Molly.

Everyone stopped walking as Molly had her mouth wide open and was confused by what Tessa had said.

Even if they changed everything, Tessa believed Marcus becoming a vampire had nothing to do with Damion and what he had made of the darkness.

Tessa continued. "All I know right now is we need to lift the curse and that starts with Yara's mother-in-law—the wicked witch, as we like to call her," she said.

Everyone continued to follow, but Molly stood there upset. *Why go back to this time when we could go even further because that could even help Danny out?* Molly thought. Maybe she could stop Marcus from being a vampire.

Austin heard what she was thinking. He placed his hand over her shoulder and helped her walk.

"If Marcus wasn't a vampire, why would he go after a werewolf and even have Danny to begin with? Be careful what you change," Austin whispered.

Molly pulled Austin's hand off her shoulders and was mad because she knew he could be right.

They arrived in front of Yara's house. In this life, her name was Laura, and she was with the man of her dreams. But his mother did not like Laura and began the story of the curse set upon a moon witch, a curse that shouldn't have happened, and now was the time to erase a part of a Gibbous witch's story that could, in fact, be undone. They had to lift the curse to save Yara and continue the journey to complete the moon spell, find the forbidden planet, and save the universe from the explosions. Every moment counted.

~ 8 ~

VOODOOISM

They all arrived in front of Laura's home. Hui pointed to the back of the house, where she spotted a man and a woman. Lucas snapped his fingers, and they were all dressed in the clothes they wore in 1579 in Tielt, Belgium. Isabel checked her pocket and couldn't find the lotion her father gave her to change their faces. Usually, they were always prepared with what they needed, but Isabel forgot the cream for the first time.

Hui told them they were moon witches and they didn't need lotion.

"Seriously? We can just change our faces?" Molly asked. "Why didn't we know that?"

"That's not your fault. After all, you still all look like children. You haven't learned as much just yet," Hui said. She closed her eyes and said the words, "Benogi Megola." She repeated it five times when their faces began to feel strange. Everyone looked at each other, feeling their own faces move as if getting a face massage with a ton of hands.

"Shit, look at you!" Austin said to Anthony.

"Okay, I get it. We look different. Pay attention and focus," Anthony replied.

"Yeah, speak for yourself. You look handsome. Take a look at Rene," Molly said as everyone started laughing.

"Oh, shut up. You don't look so good yourself," Rene said, laughing.

After a couple minutes of joking around, everyone followed Tessa when she walked into the back of the old run-down house. They saw the woman and the man arguing. Lucas told them that it was Laura and her love, Jonathan. Just as they walked closer, Jonathan sped off past them in an angry hurry.

Laura was left crying. Isabel walked closer and wanted to comfort her. Tessa held her back and whispered, "*Invali Bucanan Adyvanli.*" She said it three times when they all turned into air. They could see, but they couldn't be seen. Tessa told them to wait until they saw the evil witch.

They followed Laura into town and quickly saw a woman from afar stare at her. Laura didn't see her. They all watched as Laura began feeling pain in her arm. She then felt her heart hurt as if she was having a heart attack. People ran over to help her when the siblings and the other moon witches saw the woman in an alleyway, smiling at what was happening to Laura. Jonathan saw Laura and quickly ran to help her. The woman in the alleyway walked away from the scene. The moon witches all followed her.

They heard the lady laughing and meeting up with others. They all knew she had something to do with what happened to Laura. But what they said next confirmed it all.

"Linda will be so happy it worked," the lady said. All three of the women were walking and laughing.

Everyone looked at each other and continued following them to an abandoned house just outside
of Tielt.

"It worked! You did it! She felt exactly the pain," the lady said, going inside and walking up to a chair. The siblings snuck up to a window, following the others to watch.

The chair turned around, and they saw a woman sitting with a grin on her face. She was holding a doll. It had pins sticking out of the arm and heart of the doll. Lucas whispered that it was Linda, Jonathan's mother.

"Did you hear that?" Linda asked the ladies as she stood up.

Isabel placed her finger to her mouth, looking at Lucas. "Shh," she said quietly.

It looked like Linda was walking to the window they were near. But then suddenly, the door flew open, and Jonathan charged inside.

"Stop this, Mother. This isn't like you. I know what you're doing!" Jonathan yelled.

"Ah, my dear boy. You will soon be one of us. Damion will help you become stronger," Linda said.

"I love her, and this witchcraft must stop at once!" Jonathan said.

The women in the room started laughing as Linda yelled out that Laura was the witch, not her. She threatened to tell the townspeople who Laura really was.

Linda walked up to her son's face and told him Laura wasn't who he thought she was. She presumed she was from another planet, and soon, the world would know she was a dirty witch who needed to be punished. Jonathan yelled out his mother was crazy and she was the evil one. Linda was going to say something, but Jonathan interrupted and told her the punishment one day would be on her, not Laura. He stormed out as the women looked at Linda. Linda was furious and waved her hands as all three women fell to the ground.

"Don't give me that look. He will be begging for my forgiveness when he and everyone else see Laura as who she really is," Linda said. She grabbed the doll and stared at her creation. "A curse is nothing until it becomes a voodoo curse." She laughed as the woman began standing back up and laughing with her.

"It's the doll. You see the needle placed directly into the arm and heart where Laura was hurt." Anthony whispered.

"When I went back in time to get that necklace Rene told me to get, it was placed around a doll just like that one but the mouth was sewn shut," Molly said.

"Something sinister is going on with those dolls. We should find out more. Come, I know someone at this time who could help," Lucas said.

They walked further down, turning visible again.

"So, what happened last time you tried helping Yara?" Anthony asked.

Tessa was about to answer when more yelling was heard back at the house. They quickly turned back invisible.

They saw past Tessa and Lucas.

"To answer your question, Anthony, there we are. Quickly, let's move so we aren't seen," Tessa said as everyone sped up. "We came here before, and a fire started. We knew about the curse, but we didn't know about Zayne. She wouldn't talk much about it."

They made it to the man Lucas knew before. He was an older man with long grey hair held back with a rubber band. He dressed like a peasant. His shoes carried many holes. Lucas looked around the shop as everyone else looked at the dolls sitting on handmade wood shelves all around them. Some were black and wore seashells as clothes and feathers as hair. Others were white and stuffed with feathers inside. The outsides had a cotton fabric covering and sewn-on eyes. They all stopped and looked around as the man walked up to Molly and told her they were called Venus figurines.

He explained how the doll's images were idealized heroes or deities and very carefully modeled representations of a recognizable historical or legendary figure. He told Molly they were used for healing and to communicate with deceased loved ones. As they were both looking at all the dolls on the wooden shelf, they heard a noise coming from the back of the shop. Molly was about to look back when Lucas popped up in front of them and smiled at the older man.

"How can I help you?" the older man asked Lucas.

"Do you know who I am?" Lucas replied.

The older man looked curiously. Then he looked at Molly, and just at that very moment, everyone walked toward him.

"It's me, Lucas, well, Nickalos, as you know me," Lucas said.

"Nickalos! My right-hand man. You were just in here, and now you're back with a new face!" the older man said.

"I am—" Lucas began to say.

"From the future, I'm guessing, or is it the past?" the man interrupted.

Lucas laughed. "Yes, the future. We need your help."

"Ah, you told me you would be here, and here you are. Let me guess, you need information on a voodoo curse," he said.

"Wait, what? I told you already?" Lucas asked as everyone looked at him.

"Well, no, not you exactly. Right after you left, a boy and his father were in here. The boy told me you were coming with the moon witches," the older man said.

Everyone looked confused because now they felt like they were being watched and followed through time.

"Have you seen them before?" Molly asked.

"No, I haven't, but I knew they weren't from this time like all of you. They were dressed strangely though they definitely weren't hiding it," the man explained.

"Did they say anything else?" Anthony asked.

The man shook his head. "They were here for some doll, but the crazy part is that doll wasn't for sale. But I had an urge to give it to them—for free, too," the man said.

"Do you always give dolls away for free?" Austin asked curiously.

"Never. Got to feed my family. Ya know?"

Everyone was concerned.

"What doll did they want?" Tessa asked.

"It was a special doll that was carved from wood. That's not all, though, now that I'm thinking about it. I have a memory I didn't know I had. Does that make sense?" the older man said.

"Yes, sir. It does. Someone could have either given you a memory, taken a memory, or both," Anthony said.

"Well, it's just the father of that boy I remembered giving me the doll in the first place and told me to keep it safe even if my life depended on it. The memory just appeared as I was giving it to him," he said.

"Finn told me about a stick made from the wood of the magical trees and how Marcus hid this wood. Finn has been trying to find it," Rene said.

"You think those two were Danny and his father, Marcus, coming to get the wood that he hid here?" Anthony asked Rene.

"The last piece of wood from those trees on planet Earth might be in Marcus' hands. Great," Molly said.

"You knew these men?" the older man asked.

"We might, but that doesn't explain why they needed the wood," Rene said.

"I think we know why. Danny is a traitor, and he wanted us to know they were here," Molly said.

"Guys, you are all thinking the same thing," Austin pointed out.

"It sounds like maybe Danny and Marcus want to turn us into darkness," Rene said.

"Yes," Austin answered.

"Yeah, well, why else would they come back for a stick of wood that can harm all the moon witches?" Molly asked.

"Okay, I understand this is bad, but remember, let's help Yara. This is just another problem we are facing that can be resolved once we do the moon spell," Tessa explained.

Lucas nodded and asked his old-time friend how to stop a voodoo curse that was made with a doll. The older man showed them a book on voodoo curses. He said it could only work if they were consumed in darkness. They prepared a ritual under the moonlight that took away the doll's intentions and infused it with misfortune, pain, and even death. The maker would thrust pins into the doll as they pleaded for revenge.

The darkness then came out of the individual, causing the curse and into the doll. The older man told them it wouldn't work with a pure heart.

"So, after the darkness leaves the witch and goes into the doll, what happens to that witch?" Rene asked.

The older man turned the page and showed them the part answering Rene.

"That witch sacrifices her body. The only way they can return is if a personal item of theirs is worn by the one being cursed. That will reverse the doll's curse and bring back the body of the individual seeking revenge," he said

Anthony started pacing as he thought to himself.

"So that necklace was Linda's personal item, and she made it so the necklace couldn't be found. Did she never want to come back?" Anthony asked.

"When they are evil like that, then yes. The curse is more important than their lives. I'm just surprised you found the personal item. How did you anyway?" the man asked.

"I traveled back. It was in an old cabin in the woods," Molly said.

"Then what happened?" he said, looking worried.

"Well, a doll was inside, sitting on the fireplace right in the middle of the room. The necklace was around the doll. I kind of saw it right away because the necklace shined bright," Molly explained.

"I don't know, but that seems to be a bit easy if you ask me," the man said.

"Yeah, but she didn't know that I would dream of it and happen to have a sister that can time travel. So maybe this was fate?" Rene said.

"When hiding their personal item, it is put away with a spell even for time travelers to keep it hidden so the curse can never be broken. It is just needed to keep the curse alive," he answered.

Everyone looked at each other and began to worry about Yara.

The man looked inside the book to continue reading some passages. He paused and asked Molly what doll was it that she saw. Molly explained what it looked like. A small human puppet made with two sticks tied in a cross shape. The body had two arms sticking out as sticks. It was a brightly colored triangle of cloth.

The older man was thinking and walked to the back of
the shop. When he came back out, he was holding the same doll Molly had seen with the necklace.

"That's it! That's the one!" Molly said.

"In order to break this curse, you need to find her personal item and doll she used for the ritual," the man said as he ripped a piece of paper from the book and handed it to Lucas. "These are the words you will say and stones you need. This doll is made right by the hands of Damion himself. It is known to have his darkness inside of it. If it was out in the open, someone wanted Molly to find it and bring back the body of Damion, not Linda."

"Oh no! How do we find the real personal item?" Rene asked.

"Go now and follow the woman who prepared the ritual for the curse," the older man said.

Molly was pissed she was tricked. As they were leaving, Molly turned the corner with anger in her eyes. She went back in time to make herself never get the necklace. Without a chance for anyone to tell her no, she disappeared.

She went back to the cabin to stop herself from grabbing the necklace. When she went inside, she heard classical music playing. She hadn't heard that before. She looked around and wondered if it was the same time she had come before. Molly walked inside and turned the music off.

She yelled if anyone was there, and then the door slammed shut, and the windows locked by themselves. Molly ran and tried to get out, but she was stuck. She looked out the window, trying to open it. That's when she saw herself walk toward the cabin.

She called out to herself, but no noise was heard from the outside. Molly ran to the door to wait for herself to open it, but Molly watched herself look into the window and then just walk away. She had the necklace in her hand. *How did I get it if I didn't even walk in the house?* Molly thought.

"Fuck!" Molly screamed.

The room started to shake. It looked like the cabin was falling on its back. She then looked out a window to see what was going on as the shaking stopped. The window was now facing the sky.

She grabbed a chair and threw it at the window. Nothing seemed to work. She tried traveling but couldn't. She punched, kicked, and screamed at the top of her lungs. When nothing was working, she thought, *Where in the world am I, and why can't I get out?* Suddenly, out of the side window, she saw a huge stick as an arm and then she ran to another window and saw the feet.

"Am I Inside the doll?" Molly asked herself. She stood there in shock. She was inside the doll and couldn't get out.

***

Everyone screamed for Molly.

"Where the hell is she?" Anthony yelled.

"I don't know, she did seem pissed she was tricked," Austin said.

"Well, what was she thinking when she left?" Isabel asked.

"I don't know. I'm not listening to everyone all the time, ya know," Austin replied.

"Shoot, did she travel?" Isabel asked.

Everyone looked around as the siblings stood there, knowing their sister all too well.

"She left," Rene said as everyone agreed.

Tessa told them if it was Damion's creation, then changing it would be impossible and set up with another spell. The siblings understood, and Austin told Tessa they knew, but Molly wouldn't care and would try it anyway. Tessa thought that was careless and reckless. She thought Molly should have thought about it before going alone. The siblings rolled their eyes and told Tessa she was right, but welcome to Molly's world.

Tessa looked around and said she would have been back by now. Anthony was pissed at Molly. They tried to find her as a crescent moon power could always find each other, but this time it was different. She wasn't inside the universe. They couldn't reach her. Tessa told them that if they couldn't get to her, it was because she wasn't there. She had to be in another dimension. Anthony began making a plan. He told them they would find Linda's personal item, and when Yara could travel, they would find Molly. Even if she was somewhere else, they had the power to find it.

Everyone agreed and began running toward Linda's home. The curse was about to take place, and the siblings were not going to let that happen. They were waiting for the two items Linda brought forward, and Anthony had an idea of what he would do next.

Tessa said the spell as they all turned to air. They went toward her house and waited. They watched as Linda took her doll and began to pray, but it wasn't to a god. Instead, she used the word "Satin." The siblings all looked at each other when she was done praying to him; she put the doll on the ground and placed her hands above it.

"Thou father of all. Help me with the curse of torture and despair as you. My father will take my place inside my doll so you can be set free. I will sacrifice my soul to you, Damion, our Satin," Linda said. She took out a necklace and placed it on her doll.

They all witnessed her sacrificing everything as the necklace was placed exactly how Molly described it. Isabel told them it was happening, and that was when she said it, loud and clear, as she raised her head and closed her eyes.

"The curse will last for hundreds of years, but when the time comes and the moon witches come together, you will be free and finally kill them all," Linda said as the wind became strong inside of her home.

"Wow, it all did play out the way they wanted. The item is hers. She just completely sacrificed herself for Damion. She cannot come back, and they knew we were coming," Austin whispered.

Suddenly, a light appeared, and voices were being heard. They couldn't make out what it was saying, but it sounded like several people talking at once. Then, as Linda began to grab the doll and her necklace, she yelled out who was there. They appeared holding hands and looking toward the siblings, who were invisible to the naked eye. Isabel told Tessa to make them visible again. She and her siblings recognized who one of them was before they said anything. Linda saw the siblings and all the other moon witches appear.

Linda yelled out for all of them to leave at once, or she would cast them away. The siblings looked over at the other set of witches who appeared in the light and wind. One of them, who the siblings remembered, then spoke. He told everyone, including Linda, that they were the Quarter Moon Witches, and Yara called for their help. Everyone smiled and walked to the four bodies, who carried the quarter moon power inside of them.

They all grabbed onto each other, holding hands, when Linda saw their eyes begin to turn white. She ran out the door and into the forest.

~ 9 ~

FREEDOM

It was the moment the moon witches disappeared when Yara knew she was on her own. She ran for the necklace when it flew away from her and to the other side of the room. Yara screamed that she had found the necklace, she broke the curse, and the evil witch should stop at once. The laughter became louder and louder.

Yara tried getting out, but the door wouldn't open. Suddenly, the necklace floated into the air and brightened the room. She looked nervously and began trying magic to open the door. Knowing, she was stuck and had to face the evil witch.

In the blink of an eye, the necklace opened, and when it did, it began falling into pieces. The light disappeared, and everything went back to normal.

Yara looked around, and when she saw nothing, she ran to the necklace. It was now rusted and in pieces, as if the years of the necklace caught up to it, and the magic was no longer inside. Yara sat on her knees, wondering what happened to the necklace and what she would do without her ability to travel. Suddenly, in the corner of her eyes, she saw a shadow.

She stood up quickly and yelled out, "Who's there?" First, she heard footsteps walking toward her. Then she saw a man walk out of the shadow. Yara felt peace and was drawn to the man.

She asked who he was but couldn't shake the feeling of wanting to please the man. Yara was a strong witch who had endured pain all of her lives, but now, she felt peace and a sense of freedom. The man held out his hand without saying a word, and Yara couldn't help but hold it.

She reached, and without even touching his hand, Yara passed out and began to dream a terrible nightmare of her beatings through all the lives she had. It wasn't just a dream; she felt the pain all over again. She was forced to relive those terrible moments. She screamed but couldn't get out of the nightmare.

Suddenly, she felt as if she was thrown into the water, and within seconds, her eyes opened, and looking down at her with a bucket in her hand was Molly.

"Finally. I tried everything. You weren't waking up. How did you find me?" Molly said.

"Find you? I didn't know you were even here. Wait. Where are we?" Yara said, sitting up quickly and looking around.

"Great, so we are both stuck here. You aren't here to rescue me?" Molly asked as she threw the bucket at the window and sat on a chair, feeling a sense of defeat.

Yara ran to the door and tried opening it as Molly rolled her eyes. She asked Yara if she thought she was stupid or something. Molly told her she tried opening the door. She sat back up and told Yara to look out the windows and see where they were.

Yara began looking and couldn't believe what she was seeing. She yelled out, "We're stuck in a doll?"

She was angry and started cursing. Molly didn't say a word. Yara had been through a lot, but she dresses and looks like a calm, beautiful princess. No one has seen this side of her as she screamed.

Yara never wanted to show her son the pain she felt or the anger inside her mind. Zayne wasn't there, so she could let it out. She had tried to keep
everything bad in the world away from her baby. After she screamed for a while, she fixed herself up and looked around the place.

She took everything out of the drawers and tore the place apart. She noticed some drawers felt different than how she perceived them. Bumpy felt smooth as hard felt soft. Yara knew her eyes were seeing something other than what she was feeling. The bucket Molly had in her hand... She ran and touched the bucket. She closed her eyes and began feeling the bucket.

Molly asked what she was looking for. Yara ignored her. Molly repeated it, and once again, she was ignored. Molly ran up to her and pushed her against the wall. Even though Yara was older and taller than Molly, she still held her against the wall. Molly was angry and strong.

She yelled out inches away from Yara's face, "What are you looking for? I get you don't like to ask for help, but I was here for what seems like hours. If we work together, maybe we can get the hell out of here!"

Yara broke easily free from Molly's grip.

"If we were being held here with magic, there is something here holding the magic together," Yara said as she continued to look around.

"Okay. Makes sense, but how do you know it's here or what it could possibly look like?" Molly asked.

Yara did not answer or make eye contact with Molly as she continued looking for the object.

Molly held her tongue and took a deep breath. "What's your problem?" she asked.

"My problem? My problem? They took my ability, happiness, and overall all of my lives with that damn curse! That isn't even the biggest problem of all. They took my baby boy. Even if this all gets resolved, I had a kid! A child! I'm going to have to leave him. I messed everything up," Yara said as she fell to the ground crying.

Molly was no longer angry. She understood how Yara must have been feeling.

"I get it, Yara. After the spell the moon witches do, we aren't allowed to have a child. You did, though, and you raised a strong boy, yet here you are crying. I had a child once in another life. We are the moon witches, Yara. Once we do this spell, you will see him grow up one way or another. They can't take our happiness. We are the strongest witches ever created. We can find each other. No voodoo curse can possibly stand in our way," Molly said as she helped Yara stand up. "Now, I am here too. We have to put our minds together to get out of here."

"Minds together! That's it!" Yara screamed. She hugged Molly.

"Wait, what?" Molly said.

"We are witches; we are beyond the state of Sudhana. All we have to do is meditate and put our minds together!" Yara yelled.

Molly asked her what about the item that held the magic. Yara said this magic was from Damion, and the man who brought her there must have been him. He could only do magic with the power of an item that carried the darkness. She explained to Molly that Damion wasn't a powerful witch. He used the darkness, and if they could put their minds together, they would find what they were looking for. Molly nodded and asked what she should do. Yara took her hand and placed her in the living room.

She told Molly to sit and calm her mind. Just as the two of them began to meditate, the room shook, and everything was getting thrown around. Molly looked around, asking what was going on. Yara told Molly to focus because Damion knew what they were doing. Molly closed her eyes and tried to calm her mind and body. Everything was flying around the room. It seemed like a tornado was inside with them. Music started playing louder and louder. The two of them knew he was trying to distract them from finding what they were looking for. They noticed things were everywhere, but nothing could hurt them physically.

Even though the couch, TV, and everything flew around, nothing was touching them. Molly couldn't focus as she was nervous she would get hit with something. Yara's eyes were still closed. She yelled out to Molly to close her eyes and focus because nothing could touch them. Yara explained that Damion could not touch them. She remembered going to grab his hand when she was in her home.

Her hand hadn't touched his, and she couldn't feel his hand when she passed out. Yara yelled at Molly that none of this was real. Molly told her the bucket she felt and everything else. Yara asked her if she remembered Yara's home.

Molly sat there thinking of Yara's house. There were drawers and a single bucket of water that Yara had next to her plants. Molly had goosebumps all around her arms and legs. She asked her what was going on.

Yara yelled out they were still in her home, and everything they could touch was her belongings, but what they saw was not really there. Yara told Molly he was inside their minds, so only their minds could find the item he was using. Molly closed her eyes and began to soothe her mind.

Nothing was going to stop her because nothing was even real. It was all an illusion inside their very own mind.

Their activity in the parietal lobe slowed down. They focused their attention by funneling some sensory data in the brain, stopping other signals in their tracks.

They began working with the mind, putting effort into making it calm and clear. On the outside, their eyes were closed, and their hands were gently on their knees. Everything flying around them was moving in slow motion.

Back inside their minds, they obtained a level of spiritual realization. They felt pure love and liberation. They felt at ease and began to see what was around them.

A doll was sitting in the attic, staring at them. Molly thought as she couldn't speak, but Yara was able to understand. Molly thought they were in Yara's house right in the attic, and the doll was lying on its back, looking up at the open window. Molly asked Yara if that doll and everything here was real or an illusion.

Yara told her there was one way to find out. Yara grabbed the doll and suddenly was back in her home where she disappeared. She ran upstairs to the attic, calling Molly. She saw Molly lying down with her eyes closed and the doll sitting next to Molly's head when she walked in.

"No! Molly! Wake up! Grab the doll!" Yara screamed as she ran to Molly.

Yara escaped without Molly. She began to panic and looked at the doll. She screamed to Damion to let her go, or he would pay. That was the moment Yara saw black smoke come out of the doll and fly right out of the window. Yara shook Molly and knew Damion must have moved the darkness somewhere else. So where was Molly, and if the darkness wasn't in the doll anymore, how could Molly escape?

Yara began to move Molly's hair out of her eyes and told her she would get help. She needed her siblings to use the moon power, and the only way she could do that was if she found the other moon witches and her siblings. Yara held Molly's cheek and
told her she knew she was strong enough to hold on a
little longer. She would return and set Molly free.

Yara ran as fast as she could to find the Quarter Moon Witches. She knew where they were because she tried to stay away from one of them. His mother was the one who cast the curse centuries ago. His name was Jonathan, and he was her soulmate. Yara stayed away because he reminded her of the evil witch who ruined her lives.

Yara didn't care anymore because he was now the key to saving Molly and finding her son and siblings.

The others all traveled back to save her from the curse. She couldn't sit back when everyone was in danger because of her love for Jonathan. Yara just kept running, and nothing was able to stop her. She ran for miles and didn't stop until she reached a tiny little boat. She untied the rope holding the boat in place. Just as she was pushing the boat out, a man yelled out. He asked her what she thought she was doing and to put that back at once. He was an older man, and that was his fishing boat.

Yara jumped in and sailed away before the older man could reach her. She paddled and didn't stop until she reached land again. She jumped out and ran toward the trees. She continued until a woman jumped out, holding a bow and arrow.

"I would stop if I were you, or this arrow will go directly into your heart. Then you'll die from its venom. A slow and painful death," the woman said, pointing the arrow at Yara.

"I know who you are. Everyone knows the Quarter Moon Witches protect this side of the land," Yara said as she slowly walked toward the woman. "I wouldn't do that if I were you."

The woman stared at Yara as she walked toward her.

"Do I know you?" she asked putting down her weapon.

A man walked out of the forest toward Yara. He told her he was shocked to see her there because he knew she had been avoiding him for centuries. The woman looked at Yara. She put the arrow back in her shoulder bag. She walked toward the man.

"Is this?" the woman said as they both stared at Yara.

"Yes, it's her; it's my beautiful soulmate who ignored the universe trying to put us together," the man said.

"Together? You mean everything in its power to pull us apart. Anyway, there is no time for this!" Yara yelled out. She told them she needed the Quarter Moon Witches to help her. She wouldn't ask if it wasn't crucial. The other two witches came forward as all four moon witches were looking at Yara.

She walked closer to them and told them they had to go back in time and get her siblings back. The Quarter Moon Witches all looked at each other and nodded. Yara then looked at Philip, who once was Jonathan. She told him she had kept his secret for centuries, but she could no longer keep it because if his mother knew the truth, the love for her son would be too intense for Damion's voodoo curse. Yara yelled out to all of them that the stick Damion used to make the darkness was from the tree that the moon witches created. She told them that they were the ones to stop him.

The Quarter Moon Witches nodded and agreed. Jonathan, now named Philip, told Yara they would help bring back the others, and he would tell his mother the secret he had been keeping from her. All those years ago, Philip never told his mother he was the moon witch because he wanted to save her from Damion. He would have broken his mother into sharing that information with him because once the darkness was inside them, they began to worship Damion's evil.

If he had told his mother who he was, she would have come after her own son for Damion without knowing what she was doing. Philip knew Damion would use her to get to him and then kill her as if she was nothing.

All this time, he tried to save his mother and the love of his life, but he realized he couldn't have both. Yara told him it wasn't her in the necklace. He thought if she just found the necklace, his mother would return, and they could try and get the darkness out of her. Everyone was in shock when Yara told him it was Damion.

She said his mother must have sacrificed herself for Damion because she was gone forever, and he was the one who could come back. Philip was angry that not telling his mother his secret hadn't saved her. She still died for Damion.

They all grabbed his hand as they went back in time to face his mother. Finally, they could change what shouldn't have happened. Damion caused hell for the moon witches when he picked up that stick centuries ago. They held their hand out for Yara, but she told them she had to stay with Molly. They needed to go without her. She told them to go and save them, and when they did the spell with all the moon witches, this life would be different.

"Why will it be so different?" he asked.

Yara told him in this life, she had a son, and once the curse was lifted, her son could finally take off the sunglasses, and instead of causing fire, he would be able to see the Star Witch again. They all looked at each other in disbelief.

"With the help from the Star Witch, we can change a fixed point in time. Which means we can stop Damion from ever finding the stick and causing any of this," Yara answered.

They didn't know that could even happen. Yara told them that she had heard her boy dreaming, and she knew he'd talked to the Star Witch before, but it was never in English when it was with the Star Witch. She used magic to place it on paper and translate what was said, and when she was able to read it, it read, *The power of the trees isn't made for evil; it brings out whatever is already inside of you.*

The magical trees created to save the humans were never evil; Damion brought out his evil as it enhanced his magic and created darkness. The magic from the trees could even affect the moon witches, and Damion's intentions would turn them into his darkness. He was the one who used the magical wood for darkness. The wood itself just enhanced the magic that was inside of him.

~ 10 ~

DESTINED

Linda ran. She ran and continued running, not stopping for anyone. As if they weren't endowed with magic, she looked behind her to see if she had lost them. She hid behind a tree to catch her breath.

Holding the doll tight, she called out for Damion to stop the moon witches.

Suddenly, a light in front of her appeared. Trying to open her eyes, she appeared eager to see Damion at last. Linda smiled and bowed her head, and when she looked up, it was the moon witches—not Damion.

She yelled again for Damion, but he never appeared. Philip stepped forward as Linda stepped back in fear. Philip began to change his face for a brief moment as Jonathan.

Linda walked forward and yelled out to him that he must not carry the face of her boy. Jonathan walked toward her as she yelled for him to stop. The other Quarter Moon witches grabbed onto Isabel as she held onto her siblings. The others joined in as they all walked toward Jonathan and held his hand. Linda's mind was invaded by all the markings. She screamed, and in a mere second, Philip was in her head. He showed her the day he found out he was a moon witch.

It was the year 1562. Jonathan was thirteen years old. He was a wealthy boy but quiet and without many friends. He liked checkers, chess, and board games. The games only wealthy kids had back then. He also enjoyed nine-pin bowling and some ball games. He mostly played with adults who worked for his parents.

One day, an African American woman with a long brown dress and a hat that covered her face from the sun walked up to him as he was leaving a small white building with one room that he called school. She looked at him and took off her hat. She told him he reminded her of her Anibel. Then Linda called out his name for him to get away from her. Jonathan just stared at her as if he couldn't move.

She smiled as Linda ran to him and grabbed his arm. She told him to stay away from that crazy witch. That was the first time Jonathan heard the name witch. He looked back while his mother was pulling his arm, walking away from her. The lady smiled again and put her hat back on.

That same night, he dreamed of her standing under a full moon. She didn't speak or move; she just stood there looking at him. The next couple of months was the same dream over and over. It was only until the day he fell and cut his knee that the dream ended. He sat on the ground holding his knee when a little girl walked up to him and asked if he was okay. He looked up at the girl and told her he was fine because he didn't want help from a girl.

She giggled and sat next to him. She told him he would need the healer to make that go away. He didn't know what that meant at the time. Suddenly, the same woman that he had been dreaming about called out for her daughter.

"Anibel! Let's go, my child. Tonight is the quarter moon. Take a look, and you will see," the lady said when she saw who her daughter was talking to. "Let's go, Anibel. Before the storm."

"I will see you again soon," Anibel said as she waved, walking away.

He thought maybe his mother was right. She was a crazy witch, but that night, he couldn't resist. He snuck out of bed and walked outside very slowly and quietly. He looked up at the moon and didn't feel or see anything until he began to look away, and that's when he noticed his birthmark right on his wrist. It started glowing. He stood there in shock—scared. His mother came outside and asked if he was okay.

He hid his marking and ran inside the house. At first, he was afraid to say anything, but he noticed he was able to do things that not everyone could do.

He thought he was a freak for years until he saw Anibel again on his eighteenth birthday. She came to warn him about a darkness that was created years ago. She told him an evil man would try and turn them all into his creation. Jonathan asked who all of them were, confused about what happened to him that night and ever since.

Anibel told him she was trying to find all of the moon witches, and she had to make a spell to have them all forget who they were in every life.

"What are you saying? Am I a witch?" Jonathan asked. "Is that why I can do things I can't talk about?"

"Yes, and I'm sorry you can't remember. That's my fault. But it's time," Anibel answered.

"How is that your fault?" he asked.

"In every life we have, there's going to be a different reason we all forget. It's because of my spell. I had to. It's to keep us safe from Damion. Without it, he would find you all when you're most vulnerable," Anibel said.

"Most vulnerable?"

"Babies, tiny little things, just born. You can't protect yourself in that time, so this spell was to hide the moon witches until they were ready to fight," she explained.

When Anibel saw the look on Jonathan's face, she quickly told him the proof was with her twin sister. She was born knowing everything. She caused magic when she was a baby.

"My parents thought she was Satin's baby. Then one day, my sister was gone, and my parents pretended like she never existed. But I remembered. I knew who she was, and everyone else was wrong. Something happened, and my parents knew about it. The strange part to add to that strange part was I would see her in my dreams."

Her parents made sure Anibel wasn't a witch. They kept everything away from her that they believed could be used for magic. They didn't know the only thing she needed was the moon.

One night under a full moon, her parents were screaming at her to look and be normal, or they would give her away, too. When they said those words for the first time ever, they admitted to what Anibel already knew.

She cried and ran outside. Her mother chased her and told her to get inside now. When Anibel refused, they brought out a weird-looking doll. Anibel thought it
was strange because she had never seen that doll before. Suddenly, the doll turned into flames, and the fire grew into the trees.

Fire was everywhere. A man who now she knew was Damion came out of the fire. Anibel knew he was the one who took her sister, and she knew that not just from her intuition, but she heard her sister's screams coming from the flames. Anibel continued her story to Jonathan as he covered his mouth in shock.

She told him she ran that night and met the old lady who took her in and guided her through everything. The same lady he met that day.

"She guided me and helped me with my power. She told me never to hide, but I didn't listen. I was always so scared. I just thought Damion would take all the moon witches like he has my sister. So I wanted to hide them with the humans," she explained.

Jonathan asked why they came to him and helped him remember who he was. Anibel said the older lady had passed on to the heavenly dimension.

When she did, a woman appeared out of the heaven dimension and told Anibel never to be alone and to find the other moon witches because only together could they rescue her sister and defeat Damion once and for all.

To this day, Anibel doesn't know who the woman was, but she did exactly what she was asked. She was alone now, and she needed to tell the others who they were.

"I traveled all through time and gave one person the ability to remember and help the others, but only when they are ready to fight," Anibel said.

"I'm going to handle Damion. As for my powers, I'm not going to tell my mother. I'd rather keep her safe from all of this," he said as Anibel started walking away.

"Where are you going?" he asked.

"You might know you're a witch now. I blame the Sun Witch, but that's okay. Just practice your power, but don't think my spell has been broken. Not even the Sun Witch can break that.

You're not ready to fight," Anibel said as she walked away. "You can't break my spell until you're ready to remember everything. I'll see you then."

"Wait! Don't just go!" he yelled, but she was gone.

Anibel left and made her way around time to continue to choose that one person to help guide the moon witches.

"Hello, Blair," she said as she made her way to the person she chose for the Crescent Moon Witches. The first traveler, Blair, had never seen Molly before. When James asked her for his help with telling the siblings, it was all destined to be.

***

Philip came out of his mother's head and told everyone that Yara changed the course of the universe when she had a son and made a deal with the Sun Witch to send Abigor and change the moment they all found out they were witches.

"I didn't know what she meant by thanks to the Sun Witch. But now I do. The thing is, we know who we are, but Anibel's spell held onto the memories of what we can do. She did it as a small sacrifice to hide us from Damion until we were ready," he explained.

"I'm sick of everyone deciding what I'm ready for and using memory loss spells before I am even born!" Molly said.

"I agree with that," Isabel said.

Philip looked at his mother as all of his memories became hers.

"She's ready," he said. As soon as he did, Linda started breathing heavily because she was finally trying to fight what was inside of her. The moon witches walked around her in a circle as she sat on her knees. They all held hands around her and said some words as their eyes turned white. Their markings all began to light up, and a smoke of darkness flew out of Linda as she screamed in pain.

Philip held his mother in his arms. Without magic, she was sick and dying.

That was why she followed Damion and agreed to become his Satanist because her cancer would go away with that power. Now it was all back, and she lay on the ground dying. Philip had no idea she was sick because she also kept something from him.

"You were sick?" Philip said.

He knew she loved him. She just made a deal with an evil man to be healthy again, and the darkness made her evil.

Laura was her target, but none of that rage would have happened if not for the darkness. Philip looked up to the moon and noticed it was a crescent moon. Philip screamed at the top of his lungs when the moonlight began to get brighter and brighter. Everyone grabbed on once again and used
more moon power than they ever before. Isabel, being the healer, walked forward and began to cure his mother.

Everyone cheered, and Zayne ran up and hugged Isabel. He then spoke for the first time as he yelled out, "Mommy!"

Everyone looked as they saw Yara holding out her hands to Zayne. They hugged for what felt like forever. Everyone walked toward her. Tessa asked if they had changed the future.

Yara smiled and nodded.

Molly jumped out from behind the tree and tried to scare her siblings. Everyone hugged Molly as she screamed for them to stop. They asked her what happened, knowing that only the moon witches could remember all timelines even when they changed.

Molly said she just appeared back outside where the angel statute used to be, but now it was not. Yara smiled and told them the curse didn't happen. Everyone cheered again, but this time, all grabbed onto Yara and started hugging her and Zayne.

Molly told them someone was still trapped in that doll. Everyone looked at her. Still remembering everything, she remembered Yara leaving her as she grabbed onto the doll. But when Molly grabbed it instead, she was brought to a mirror.

"There was a girl stuck in the mirror," Molly explained. When she tried to help her, the girl disappeared.

Philip asked how old she was. Molly wasn't sure; she said the girl was very young, maybe about four. Molly said the girl just looked at her without moving a muscle, but a single tear appeared from one eye and ran down her face.

Everyone seemed concerned while Molly told them she had some sort of marking, like a circle on her forehead.

Philip asked what exactly did it look like. Molly told them it looked like all of their markings, except hers, looked like the full moon.

~ 11 ~

THE MAGIC SCHOOL BUS

December 1st, 2022, They were all back inside their home. Except this time, they had all the moon witches with them except for the pure full moon witches. Rene and Molly used a powerful spell years ago in another life to carry the full moon power inside of them, but it wasn't pure. It was a spell that created the werewolves under the full moon.

There was a powerful witch that was made when the moon power spread into each phase of the moon.

Two souls were formed, and they were twins. They looked identical and did not turn into werewolves because they were the purest full moon power witches.

Ladle came out with tea for everyone. They all wanted to reach the full moon witch. Philip had met Anibel once before, and now he knew where her sister was. Hui told them that they had the power to reach her. Everyone agreed because their power could only grow from here.

Ladle and Tessa set up the candles. Each candle helped them all concentrate.

The moon witches held hands and began to feel their souls lift up into the sky. They were able to see the ground below them as people looked like tiny little ants crawling around. In the distance, they saw a light beam up and shine through the sky. They all thought a single thought of going toward the light, and without any movement, they were there.

It wasn't blocks away as it had seemed but thousands of miles and across the ocean. When they arrived, in front of them was an abandoned bus in the heart of Alaska.

They weren't really there, only in their minds, but to their surprise, the bus door opened and out popped a lady.

"I'll see you soon," she said as she and the bus disappeared.

The meditation was interrupted by the microwave.

"Sorry, Ladle said as she ran to the kitchen. She came back out with some pizza rolls. "So, did you find her?"

"Yes, actually we did," Austin said as he, Lucas, and Molly all dug into the pizza rolls. "She is living out of a bus, but not just any bus. It kind of looked like from that show the *Magic School Bus*."

Right away, Anthony knew exactly where it was. He turned on the TV and went to the documentaries. Molly laughed and told him they didn't want to watch his stupid documentaries.

Anthony went to search for a specific one that was about a man who left everything behind and traveled to Alaska. He lived off the land, and there in the movie clip was the bus they'd seen. Anthony told them that the bus saved him and was randomly kept in the middle of nowhere. Everyone looked at each other and knew that was where the full moon witch was.

Yara told Zayne to stay with Ladle, and she would return.

Her main concern was that Zayne wouldn't get hurt because she didn't know what to expect there. The teleportation spell was used after they dressed in warmer clothing. As soon as they arrived, the place looked exactly as they had seen it, except for the bus. It wasn't there.

"Where the hell is it? It was right here," Molly said, waving her hands in the spot they saw it.

Everyone looked around as it started snowing lightly.

"Well, let's see if anyone knows anything about the bus we saw," Anthony said. They all started walking to find anyone in sight.

They ended up miles away. "I don't think anyone would be up at this time, let alone find a store that'll be open," Rene said.

"Spoke too soon, buttercup," Molly replied, pointing to a store down the road.

The lights were on so they all headed to the shop. Walking inside, they all started looking around as normal as possible. The store clerk was staring at them as soon as they walked in, just knowing they weren't from around there.

"Can I help you?" he said.

"We are here on a family vacation, and we wanted to see the bus from that documentary," Austin said as he heard the clerk's thoughts and knew he had his hand on a gun below them. He also knew the man knew everyone around.

"Ah yes, that bus. That is the magic bus that so many people try and reach, but many have died trying as the wind and cold can kill a man, especially up that mountain. You don't look like mountain climbers to me. I wouldn't try if I were you," the man said.

"I'm sure someone can help us," Isabel said as Austin heard someone in the back of the store.

"Well, my brother has seen it with his own eyes, but he is mute and wouldn't talk to anyone. But they moved that bus I heard from gossip around town and took it away maybe to a museum somewhere anyways," the man said as a door slammed from the back of the store.

Austin asked if that was his brother back there. The man put his hand back on the gun and told them to go because his brother wouldn't talk to anyone.

They all looked at each other and nodded. Tessa thanked him for his time. She explained they were just curious, but they would be going back now to get some sleep. The man nodded and stood there watching them leave.

"Well, that was pointless," Molly said outside.

"Austin, what did you hear in there?" Anthony asked.

"Well, other than the man ready to shoot at anything we said suspicious, he was telling the truth. But his brother was definitely in the back because I heard him thinking he needed to run from us," Austin explained.

"Let's go find him," Hui said. They all ran toward the back of the shop.

Minutes went by as they split up searching.

"Guys, over here!" Hui shouted. "We will not hurt you," she said to the man. "We just need to find that bus."

The man looked scared and shook his head. He placed his hands on his ears and kept shaking his head.

The others ran up to them and looked at him. Isabel knew he was scared, feeling his energy and began to feel scared herself. She lifted her hand to him and asked if he was okay. When he looked at her, he calmed down and started pointing to the mountain where the bus once stood. Isabel asked him where it had gone. But he continued to point and not say a word.

Austin looked up at the mountain and told them he was thinking it was there. The man was shocked that Austin knew what he was thinking. He started pointing and jumping up and down.

"Um, what's he thinking now, all excited like that?" Molly asked.

Austin stood, quietly looking at him.

"Hello, Austin? What's he thinking?" Molly asked again.

"He is excited to meet another mind reader," Austin answered.

"Another?" Rene asked.

"Yeah, he is thinking how me and the witch up there can now both hear him."

The man smiled and clapped his hands.

"So he knows who she is," Lucas asked.

Austin didn't have to answer. The man was nodding over and over again.

"She made a spell to not be seen. She is up there," Austin said. "Oh, and he says she is waiting for us."

They all stared at the mountain as Austin thanked the man for helping.

Arriving back on the mountain, the wind and snow were progressing. When reaching the top where the bus should be, they held hands and closed their eyes.

The moon was getting brighter and brighter and began to light up the mountain. The bus appeared as the moonlight shone in the exact spot. Philip yelled out for her to come out. The lights inside the bus turned on, and when it did, the bus fully reappeared.

The door started to open just as they saw it before.

She was an older lady with grey and black hair. Wrinkles were only seen under her eyes. The fur skin she wore looked as if it had been hunted and sewn within the day. She seemed like she could survive in the wild without any help or much to work with.

"Come. Come in," the full moon witch said.

"Anibel. You remember me?" Philip asked. "My name is Philip now, but it was Jonathan."

"Ah, yes, but you all shouldn't have to change your names. As mine has always been Anibel."

"What do you mean?" Lucas asked.

"I was the one who made you all forget who you are. The lives have always been different for you all, but no matter how strong my spell was, the universe is always stronger. Remembering is inevitable," Anibel said.

Philip explained they knew why she did it as he told them what she shared with him all those years ago. Anibel looked at Lucas and told him he was the only one that could remember his lives as little as a child, and she didn't know why until she met the Star Witch.

Confusion was in most of their eyes, so she started to explain a little more.

She told them she tried to save them from Damion, and when seeking a spell, she found a book on Mount Shasta. Her dreams had led her there. Rene asked her if she knew about that mountain. Anibel looked down to the ground in disappointment. She told them she thought it was made to help them, but instead, it was to trick her because the Sun Witch knew that with her spell, none of them would have the memory to remember who they were. She was used, Anibel explained.

Yara asked to see the book, and when Anibel went to grab it, Yara looked nervous. She held the book in her hands when Anibel gave it to her.

"Guys, remember I told you I used a spell to also alter your memories to wait longer because I was not ready to leave my body until I lifted the curse from my boy?" Yara said.

Everyone remembered that as they nodded.

"This is the same book I got the spell from."

Yara turned straight to the page as she knew exactly where it was. She held up the page she'd used years ago to bring Abigor to this universe and make the Crescent Moon Witches forget who they were. Yara told them it was only supposed to last a year at most, but she also was fooled.

Anthony asked Yara to see the book. He looked inside and saw spell after spell after spell, but they were all made strictly for the moon witches' memories. Rene said that if it was found on that mountain, then maybe it was put there on purpose because during the shift, that mountain opened, and the parallel universe was on the other side.

"I found a spell to save you from Damion, but only until you all were able to fight him and Yara found the same book to use it, gaining more time to save her son. Both of us were used because we both fell for a spell to erase the moon witches' memories," Anibel said now coming to realize she and Yara had been tricked.

> She continued to say that a planet was hidden
> with a spell because that planet was made from pure
> magic.

Anthony said yes, it was the forbidden planet they needed to remember. Anibel explained that the planet was a world that connected all three witches—Sun, Moon, and Star. She was able to seek guidance from the Star Witch because of her marking. She showed everyone her full moon marking. It was given to them when they collided with the single world that started the Big Bang. Anthony asked if that planet of magic had the magical trees.

Anibel smiled, and she told them that those trees were created from each consciousness that evolved and became a powerful witch. When all consciousness made it to that planet, it became their home, a place called Larslnazm.

Everyone looked confused because even Lucas couldn't remember. Anibel told them it was time to remember everything, but there was one more person they needed. They would have to go back in time and use her power because she couldn't be found.

They had tried so many times before. Philip knew who she was talking about because he quickly interrupted and told Anibel they knew where she was. Anibel looked confused and told them they were never able to find her in all of their lives. They always had to go back in time and use her power from the past. Philip looked at Yara and then back at Anibel. He told her that Yara had changed everything because she had a son in this life, and it caused a reaction in time because now they had witnessed Damion's power as it lay in his dolls.

Anibel asked what he meant by that. Molly told her she had seen her sister, and Lucas had shared with all of them that they had never been able to see her before.

Damion had a hold on her, but she wasn't really in his doll—only her mind was. Her body is somewhere in this 3D world. Anibel told them they would have found her if she had been here. Yara thought about it, and as everyone was talking, she picked up the book and started frantically looking. Isabel noticed and nudged Rene as everyone else noticed and looked.

Hui asked what she was looking for. Yara didn't know exactly but continued to flip through the pages. Anibel asked her why she thought it would be inside that book. She was inside Yara's mind and knew what she was thinking. Austin also heard and told everyone Yara felt if they couldn't reach the other moon witch, it was because she wasn't in this universe.

She looked and looked as Molly thought about it and told them she thought Yara was onto something because the girl wasn't inside the house where Molly was but instead in the mirror as if it was a window to the other universe. Suddenly, the words in the book started mixing up and moving. Yara held it up and told them to all look at what was happening. The whole group began trying to figure out what was going on. There was a sudden halt to the words as Isabel read it out loud.

"We have a lead hurry back. Graham left a message we believe it is for all of you to find, Amanda," Isabel read.

"Now? Horrible timing. We have to find the other moon witch," Molly said.

Anibel walked to her door and opened it. She told everyone, "Or perfect timing as everything happens for a reason, does it not?"

~ 12 ~

ENDURANCE

The moon witches all made it back to New Orleans. They met up with Amanda and the wolves. Amanda didn't waste any time; she ran up to them and handed Austin the note. She told him it had Austin's name on it. He read the letter out loud.

Austin,

When you get this, I will no longer be in New Orleans. I have found a lead on finding my father. We can get to the magical planet with the help of a real live angel. She holds the key to unlock the magical planet where my father is held. We believe she was Damion's love child, and the only way to find her is the blood of her father.

The witches of New Orleans tried to track her down before, and they believed a spell was put in place to keep her hidden.

Tell Molly I'm sorry, but Danny is with Marcus, and we are following them because they are the ones bringing Damion back.

P.S. go to the woman in the library. She will show you the map to where Danny and Marcus are headed next. See you there.

- Graham

Everyone stood there thinking as Molly picked up a rock and threw it, screaming at the top of her lungs. The birds from the trees flew away from the scream. Isabel told them that if Graham was following them, they have to catch up to them before Damion returns. Rene agreed and said since they changed the timeline and that curse never happened, Damion never returned, so he was either dead or somewhere else.

"Well, he's about to be brought back once again," Hui said.

"He was always, one way or another. We have to deal with stopping him," Anibel said.

Everyone knew by now that Damion was evil. Anthony told them to follow. They all had to head to the library to find the woman and get the map they needed. Austin and Isabel looked at each other and
wondered if it was the same woman they had met before.

As they all walked away, Amanda asked what else they needed from her and the wolves. Anthony turned around and told her they would handle this but thanked them for their help. Amanda smiled and bowed her head. She and the wolves ran off into the forest as their search for Graham came to an end. Before they walked completely away, Molly yelled back and asked where they found the note. Amanda told her it was given to her by a vampire Graham must have trusted.

Everyone turned around and wondered who.

"His name was Finn, and he has been helping Graham track down Marcus," Amanda yelled back.

Austin looked at the note again, saying that Graham mentioned the word "we" as he wrote the letter. Which meant someone was with him.

Amanda yelled back before she went further into the forest that Finn mentioned there were three of them.

As they arrived at the library, they were all thinking about who the third person was but knew they were all following Danny and Marcus and had to get there before the spell to bring back Damion.

As soon as they all walked inside, they didn't want too many people walking to the back of the library and being noticed or looked at, so they split up as Lucas, Yara, and Molly went to the bookshelves to the left, and Tessa, Hui, and Rene went to the right. Anthony, Austin, Philip, and Isabel went straight ahead. A woman behind the counter saw them. She followed Anthony, Philip, Austin, and Isabel to the back as the other Quarter Moon Witches watched outside just in case this was a trap.

Seeing the lady, Anthony was going to say something, but right away, she closed the door behind them with her mind.

They knew that power as their mother carried the same ability the lady did. Isabel asked if she remembered them. The lady looked at her and Austin and smiled. She told them that she knew they would be back, and she would see them again. Anthony introduced himself, but she already knew who they were.

"You are the moon witches, and Graham has filled me in with all of his friends. Anthony is the leader and strength of the siblings. Rene is a wise woman who can also lead in a time needed with her quick thinking. Molly is the brave and outspoken, honest sibling. Ah, and you two, Austin, the loyal friend, and Isabel, the hot, kind-hearted beauty. Those are Graham's words exactly," the lady said as Isabel blushed and Austin laughed.

"That's definitely us. Well, IDK about the hot part," Anthony said as Isabel nudged his arm.

"I'm flattered he said that about me, but we are here for something more important than flattery," Isabel said, still blushing.

"Yes, the map. I dreamt of this map and told the three of them about my dream. Graham told me to write it down and save it for all of you. This is where I believe Marcus and his son are headed. That's where Graham and his friends will be," the lady said as she handed Isabel the map she had drawn out for them.

"Thank you. We have to go find them," Isabel said as she hugged the lady and thanked her again.

The lady told them that after her dream, she looked up the place on the computer and saw their history with a voodoo witch named Mollie Crenshaw and asked them to be careful. They all took a deep breath. They were headed toward another voodoo witch because even though the curse never happened, Damion still created the darkness with the magical tree centuries ago. On the way out, Austin asked the lady who the other person with Graham was, other than Finn. The lady told them that her name was Elana, and she was a human.

They all looked at each other, wondering who she was and why she was helping Graham. They all thanked her again and walked directly out the door as the others walked behind them. Rene asked where they were going and what did the map say. Isabel told her they were headed to Missouri because that was where Graham would be dealing with another voodoo witch.

They used a teleportation spell to arrive in Missouri as fast as they possibly could. Austin asked where they should look first. Isabel and Anthony were staring at the map when suddenly Molly pointed in the distance and told them they should start where the screaming and running kids.

Everyone looked and saw what Molly was pointing to. Teenagers were running out of the woods, so they all ran toward them.

"What's wrong?" Anthony asked the teenagers.

The kids started laughing and told Anthony nothing as they ran away. The moon witches looked at each other and heard more screaming coming from the woods where the kids were running from.

They all ran toward the screaming. When they arrived, they saw a boy tied to a grave. Anthony, Hui, and Lucas all started to untie the kid as Rene asked what had happened. The kid must have been fifteen or sixteen. He had blue eyes and blonde hair with freckles all over his face.

"They always bully me. I was scared of walking past the woods on my way home, and they knew I was scared. They held me down and tied me up," the boy said.

"Are you kidding me? Those are bullies? They'll get what's coming to them," Molly said as she began to plan something.

"Why were you scared of the woods? It's a beautiful part of nature. Nothing to be afraid of," Rene said.

As Anthony untied him, he sat up and told them it was because of the witch who haunted this forest. Before asking any more questions, as the boy stood up, they saw whose grave it was. It read, *Miss Mollie J. Crenshaw 1861-1913.*

Everyone stood there staring at the grave. The boy told them that she wasn't just under her tombstone. She was scattered piece by piece all over that area of the woods. Everyone looked around them at the ground. The boy thanked them for helping him, but he had to go back now before his mother worried. Tessa asked how he knew about the witch. The boy replied that everyone knew the story of the voodoo witch in his town. As the boy ran away, Isabel stared at the map.

"Guys, I think that's where we were supposed to go," Isabel said as she looked at the map and began to turn it sideways. "Well, here, but more like that way," she said as she pointed further into the woods.

Everyone looked at where Isabel was pointing but didn't see anything but trees. Tessa told them to follow, if the map said that way, then they had to go that way. Everyone followed as Tessa and Isabel led the way.

They all walked to the very spot the map showed. They looked around but didn't see anything. Philip held out his hands and told them magic would find them. Suddenly, as they began to grab on, they heard voices coming from a few feet away. With too many people, Tessa quickly said some words and they turned invisible. When they did, they saw Finn behind the tree a few feet away from them. He was able to see them.

He held his finger to his mouth, telling them to be quiet. They all stood still and watched as Danny and Marcus stood right before their eyes. Molly gasped in disbelief. When Danny looked toward them, Rene held Molly's mouth and stood completely still. Danny turned back around and walked away with Marcus. When they were further out in the distance, Molly pushed Rene's hand away. She then started running toward Finn.

"What's going on? We should have shown ourselves all of us against those two. They wouldn't have a chance," Molly said.

Anthony said they would, and he asked Finn where Graham was.

Finn took Rene's hand and kissed it gently, then he told them to follow him. Rene smiled and blushed as everyone began to follow. As they ran the opposite
way of Danny and Marcus, Finn told Molly not to

worry. They had been tracking them down for a while now, and this was where they would be because tonight, on the full moon, was when they would resurrect Mollie and bring back Damion.

"Wait, so we are letting them resurrect a voodoo witch and letting them bring back Damion before we do something?" Isabel asked.

Finn explained that Mollie was Damion's love. Marcus planned to use her for his own agenda, and Damion wasn't dead. Instead, he had been waiting inside a doll that lived on the other side of the mirrors, and they had reason to believe it connected to the parallel universe.

The siblings knew they'd changed things when stopping the curse but realized Damion hadn't come back from a necklace. Now, he was hidden where the moon witches couldn't go—inside the mirror.

Molly said they had to stop that then, shouldn't they? Before Finn could answer, they saw Graham jump from high up in the tree and reply to Molly.

"No, we have to let them bring back Damion in order to stop him. Plus, Damion is needed to find the angel. She can show us where the magical planet is," Graham said.

"Who is this angel, and why her?" Anthony asked.

"I'm not sure. Ask yourselves that question. The Crescent Moon Witches gave her the key to the magical trees. With her help, the planet will appear, and I can save my father."

Everyone looked at the siblings. They didn't remember the angel or the spell—nothing.

"Graham, we need to save the last moon witch so we can remember everything. Then we wouldn't need to find this angel," Isabel said.

A girl jumped down from another tree. She was utterly camouflaged, and no one knew she was there this whole time. Everyone jumped from the surprise.

"Damion has prisoners in the mirrors, and when they bring back Damion, all we have to do is somehow get his blood and his right index finger so we can do the spell to find the angel. Then you all can get the magic stick and place it in his heart. Then and only then can the prisoners be free. The last moon witch is one of them, so don't you see this is all connected? We all need to get Damion back to get what we want," the girl said.

"Everyone, this is Elana. Elana, this is everyone," Graham said.

Isabel blushed as Graham smiled at her, knowing what he'd said about her.

Graham looked at Austin. "I'm happy to see you all again," Graham said. Austin pulled him into a hug and they did their handshake.

Elana waited for a moment so they could say their hellos, but soon after, she wanted everyone to focus. She said at precisely 3:00 am, they would begin the spell, and they all needed to be ready because if Damion stepped out of the circle of stones, it would be too late. They had to get his blood and finger while he was still in the stones.

Isabel asked why. Elana told her he would be most vulnerable when he first appeared, and that was when they would get what they needed and when the moon witches could use the stick to bring back the innocent people he had trapped in the mirrors. Once he left the stones, his complete power of the stick would make it easy for him to escape into their world.

Anibel quickly thought of her sister. She told them they had to be ready, so they could not only save the last moon witch but also find the planet. The Crescent Moon Witches hid from everyone and gave the key to an angel they couldn't remember at all. The memory was placed away, hidden in their minds, where they couldn't have access even if they tried. They all waited in a cabin that was invisible to every human and witch.

They waited until 3:00 a.m., gathering what they needed to overpower Damion, Marcus, and, sadly, Danny.

As time was coming closer, Austin heard what Graham was thinking.

"Graham, why don't you tell everyone who you think the angel was. We still have time," Austin said, looking at the clock.

Graham smiled because he'd missed his friend, the mind reader.

"Well, we need his blood and finger because we believe the angel is his daughter," Graham explained.

"Ah, the love child you said. But wasn't Marcus his only child? Why do you think that? And if you're right, why the hell would we trust her to give us access to the planet we were hiding?" Anthony asked.

Graham shrugged his shoulders and told them Damion didn't raise the angel. He wanted nothing to do with her. They found documents, and it looked like it was all true. He explained she was left alone when her mother passed away and was brought by her mother straight to the heaven dimension and became an angel.

"Did she die, too?" Isabel asked.

"No, that's the thing. Her mother was, and she brought her living daughter there, and that little girl was the only one alive to ever grow up in that dimension," Finn said.

Anibel said she believed that might be who she saw in the heavenly dimension. Graham walked up to her and asked whether she was sure it was her. Anibel explained she was the only figure there not glowing because everyone else was made of light. She was a figure different from the others. She heard voices but couldn't make out what anyone looked like except the woman. Elana jumped as she was putting salt in a potion bottle.

"That was her! She never died. She was placed there by her mother. So her figure looks like human form!" Elana exclaimed.

"Did she say anything?" Finn asked, leaning up against the doorway.

"Well, she wanted me to find all the other moon witches," Anibel said.

Elana was so excited because she always wanted to see the angel. They all looked at each other, knowing exactly what they had to do, and they even felt a sense they were moving in the right direction. For the first time since this began, Anibel knew she was
getting her sister back. It was just in a matter of
hours.

"Wait, so were you invisible back there or we couldn't see you from that camouflage outfit? We heard you were a human," Isabel said to Elana.

"I have a gift that has nothing to do with power. I'm a human, though," she said.

"So, how do you know so much about this, and why are you helping?" Isabel asked.

Elana and Graham looked at each other as they then looked at Finn. Elana told them that she grew up hunting so she could hide in plain sight. Graham nudged her to continue explaining.

She looked back at everyone and said her ancestors were witch hunters.

The moon witches took a step back, except Isabel. She squinted her eyes and asked what happened as she felt safe around Elana. Elana told her that her grandmother was adopted about seventy-five years ago. Isabel asked what her name was—her grandmother. Elana told her it was Madeline. Isabel looked shocked as Molly asked her if she knew her. Isabel asked if she knew her birth name before adoption.

As soon as Elana said the word Nolan, Isabel hugged her. Elana wasn't a hugger, just like Molly. Anthony and Rene looked at each other as they knew Nolan was Shelby's family name.

Isabel told Elana her grandmother was adopted from their family.

"What? No, you all are the strongest witches ever created," Elana said.

Isabel laughed. "Our grandmother was actually a witch hunter even though she had a son who was the strongest warlock in Altair."

Elana was shocked and said when all this was over, they should meet her grandmother because she
was the one who told her about witches. She would be the one to know if that was true.

The siblings looked at each other. They were happy to hear she left witch hunters and instead was adopted by a family that helped the witches.

Isabel knew she had met her already when she was a little girl in Roswell, New Mexico but promised the others would all meet her soon enough.

Three a.m. was getting closer. Molly was ready to see Danny face to face as her anger at the betrayal felt like fire was burning her blood. She never thought he would become evil and set Damion free. They all grabbed everything and stayed invisible.

Finn, Elana, and Graham walked first as they weren't giving up their mission. The moon witches waited further back for Damion to appear, and then they would use the moon power to take the very sick Danny. Marcus would have to resurrect Mollie, the voodoo witch.

~ 13 ~

RESURRECTION

The time was three o'clock in the morning, and the siblings could feel the vibration of the ground below them. Something was happening, and the feeling was far from pleasant.

The moon witches waited behind the trees until Graham was able to get what he needed. Graham, Elana, and Finn got into position when Danny and Marcus stood on the grave of Mollie Crenshaw.

Danny seemed nervous to Graham, but when Graham whispered that to Elana, she told him he was lost and not the same person he once knew. She told Finn and Graham to focus as she pulled out a small crystal ball. Graham asked if that was what the witches in New Orleans made to collect Damion's blood and finger.

Elana nodded and looked toward Danny and Marcus while biting her bottom lip. Graham and Finn looked at each other, remembering that when Elana lied, she was actually terrible at it.

Elana not only had a slight twitch in her left eye. The moment she lied about something, but she also bites her bottom lip.

"Why are you lying?" Graham asked.

She stood by her words. "I'm not," she said. "It's to help get what I need."

"You mean what we need—as in all of us?" Finn questioned.

Elana laughed it off. "Yes, man. That's what I meant."

She held the ball toward the grave and told them to relax and focus on the mission. Graham and Finn looked at each other and tried to brush off the feeling that Elana was hiding something from them. Danny and Marcus stood over the grave and began to place the stones around. Two sets of stones were placed in a circle as the moon witches walked closer little by little. That was when Molly had a good view of Danny.

She began breathing heavily as Rene told her to calm down or she would blow their cover. Molly ignored Rene and wanted to knock Danny down. Suddenly, Marcus began to set fires all around them as he held up the stick and yelled for Danny to get ready.

Marcus screamed the words, "Delvan espono meogroso." Danny joined in as his father handed him the stick. "Delvan espono meogroso," they yelled out.

Flames got heavier and taller as they continued saying those words, holding up the stick. Everyone watched as Danny walked over to each circle of stones and placed a doll inside one, and when he walked over to the other one, Amanda and the other wolves that were sired to Danny appeared out of nowhere, snatched Isabel up, and threw her into the other set of stones.

Everyone was panicking as they watched Isabel being pulled from a group of wolves. The invisibility was no longer working. The siblings screamed and ran toward Isabel. Finn yelled out to Rene to get back, but the siblings didn't care. They continued to run toward her.

Isabel was screaming and tried to get out but couldn't pass the stones. Marcus started laughing, and he told Danny to get them back. Danny whistled, and the vampires came and grabbed all the moon witches, Graham, Elana, and Finn. There were hundreds of vampires and werewolves holding them down. Rene yelled at Amanda to set them free. Amanda couldn't resist the control Danny had over her. She stood there as her body wouldn't move, but her eyes were screaming with sorrow.

"You thought we didn't know you were all coming? We needed you here to you watch your sister's power gets sucked right out of her body, and the power of healing will help us set Mollie free!" Marcus yelled as he started laughing. His evil laugh vibrated into their ears.

"How could you do this, Danny? Why are you letting your father control you!" Molly screamed out as two vampires were holding her down.

Danny wouldn't look at Molly. Marcus yelled out for the vampires to shut her up. The vampires placed pressure on Molly's neck. Graham watched as Danny slighting cringed when Molly was choked and held down. She spit out blood from trying to break free and being hit in the face.

Anthony was held down by seven men and still felt like he could set himself free. He looked around and then saw Anibel staring at him. She spoke telepathically for Anthony to wait, and when Damion appeared, Graham would move fast, get what he needed, and then he would break free and run as fast as he could to the stick and place it inside Damion's heart. Anthony gently nodded his head in agreement.

Marcus told Danny to place the stick down. Danny nodded and placed the stick in between Isabel and the doll outside of the stones. Danny looked at Isabel as she stared at him, feeling something was off. He then looked at Amanda as she nodded her head.

Graham and Finn were able to see Danny perfectly. They wondered if Danny was up to something else.

Suddenly, the stick and the stones began to light up as Danny took a step back. Marcus was continuing the words over and over again. The doll began to rise as Isabel screamed in pain. Anthony wanted to go now when he heard his sister scream. Anibel told him to wait until Damion appeared. She reminded him that
nothing was final until he walked out of the stones.

Molly tried traveling, but it seemed impossible for her to focus, and she felt as if she was going to pass out instead.

Crenshaw was being raised from the dead as Isabel fell to the ground, and her power was sucked out of her and into Crenshaw. The power of Mollie Crenshaw completed the spell, and Damion began to form into a human body right before their eyes. Everyone couldn't believe the man who created the darkness was right there in front of them, knowing his followers called him Satin. Graham watched Elana stumble as if too nervous now to carry out her plan with the crystal ball. She held it in her hand, hesitating to use it. Graham yelled what she was waiting for. Elana looked at Isabel and then at all the moon witches being held down and screaming.

Elana looked at Graham and dropped the crystal ball as it shattered to the ground.

Everyone saw what she had done. Anibel yelled out to Anthony now. That was when Anthony stood up high and fought the vampires off of him. But before he could get the stick, Danny picked it up, and Amanda ran to grab Isabel and pull her out of the stones. Marcus looked at Danny in anger, and before he could do anything, Danny stuck the stick from the magical tree and placed it inside Damion's heart. The vampires and werewolves let everyone go and walked toward Marcus.

Marcus screamed at Danny in disappointment, and before the darkness lifted from inside Marcus, he could do one more thing. He raised the fire and made it spread through Danny. Danny was burning alive as Marcus fell to the ground, and what looked like black smoke came out of Marcus and disappeared.

The moon witches gathered around to help Danny as his father left him burning in the fire. After putting the fire out, they all grabbed hands and looked up to the moon. Even Molly joined in to help Danny. Anthony grabbed Isabel as she was waking up. As soon as she saw Danny screaming in pain, she told Anthony she was fine. They had to help him at once. When they grabbed on, the moon began to light up all the vampires and werewolves stared at what was happening. Amanda watched as Danny was dying slowly and painfully. It seemed the fire was too big and strong. He'd burned too much to survive.

Marcus stood up and realized what he had done. Finn ran and grabbed onto Marcus just in case he wanted to make a run for it, but Marcus didn't want to run. He yelled for the witches to save Danny as he fell to his knees, regretting what he had done.

Graham saw Elana crying on the ground. He stood next to her because he knew she was hiding something. The moon witch's markings began to light up as their eyes turned white. Everyone else watched as the doll that was placed inside the stones broke apart into tiny pieces, and a small little wormhole formed and became bigger and bigger.

The moon witches continued as everyone else was watching people step out of the wormhole. A little girl with a marking on the middle of her eyebrows walked out. Her marking began to glow the closer she walked to the moon witches.

That little girl grabbed onto Isabel and Anthony, and when she did, her eyes turned white like the others. The fire all around the forest quickly disappeared, and Danny's burns were completely gone.

Amanda and Graham ran to him to make sure he was okay. Danny looked at his body and couldn't believe he felt perfectly fine after feeling his body being burned from the outside in. He told them he was okay, thanks to the moon witches. Everyone looked at the witches when suddenly a light shined from the sky all the way to the middle of the circle the witches made when they were all holding hands.

"All the moon phases are together," Graham said.

"This is so epic," Amanda said.

The rest of them watched as a beautiful woman appeared inside of the circle, and the light faded away. The woman was an angel, and Graham, Finn, and Elana looked at each other as right before their eyes, the angel they had been searching for stood.

She told them as she sparkled in the moonlight that her father's darkness was finally gone with the evil that was inside of it. She held out her hand as Marcus floated toward her.

"My brother, it wasn't your fault. I'm giving you a choice you must make. Do you want to live as this creature for all eternity, or would you come with me into the heaven dimension?" the angel said.

Marcus looked at Danny and smiled. He told him he had lived many years. He was so sorry for all he had put him through. That was never his true self. Danny understood and nodded his head.

The angel waved her hand, and a little liquid in a clear tube appeared in the hands of the vampires and werewolves.

"One sip," the angel said, "and you will all become human again." But she warned them that when becoming human, they had to all become enlightened and never forget the magic they witnessed.

Some drank right away, but others hesitated. Amanda didn't know what she should do. She enjoyed being a werewolf, but then again, that was all she knew.

Finn and Rene locked eyes, thinking if he became a human, he would grow old with Rene and always

be her age as their lives continued to find each

other.

Finn drank it without another doubt as Danny looked at it, not knowing what he should do.

He looked at Molly, but she was still locking hands with the witch's. Their eyes were pure white. He knew she couldn't hear him. He placed it in his pocket because he didn't want to make the choice just yet. The angel smiled and told them the choice was theirs. She held hands with her brother, and when she did, Marcus's body fell as his soul continued to stand. Danny yelled out to ask if he would always remember his father. The angel nodded and told him he would remember him as he truly was before he turned evil. She placed memories of his father's true self into Danny that were way before Danny's time.

She smiled and said he would remember him as a vampire who fell in love with a werewolf because that was what he would have done. The angel explained that he made the Crescent Moon Witches always keep an eye on him every time he was reincarnated. She continued to say only good will happen now that the evil was gone. Marcus and the angel turned into the light and rose into the sky as they faded away above the stars.

The moon witches open their eyes and looked at each other. They just knew out of nowhere that the key they placed upon the angel was Zayne. He is the one who had to gather the star, moon, and Sun Witch, and he was the one who could reach the planet made of magic. The angel left that very memory in each of their minds before she left. They all looked at Yara as she smiled and told them she knew he was a miracle and was given to her as a gift from the universe, and that was exactly what he was.

The boy was the key to the planet, and when they saved Graham's father, they would be ready to meet the Star Witch and erase Damion from ever grabbing that stick.

***

Ladle heard noises coming from Zayne's room. She quickly walked to his bed to make sure he was okay. Zayne was sound asleep miles away from the moon witches, yet his dream was coming on strong. Ladle watched as his eyes began to twitch and his fingers started to wiggle. Ladle saw he was just dreaming and sat there beside him to make sure he was okay. Inside Zayne's dream, he was climbing a mountain and when he got to the top, he looked down and saw billions of trees. They all have markings on them of different symbols.

A man with a disfigured face and green moles all over his body and sharp scales on his arms was running from further away and stopped below the mountain, he looked up at Zayne and asked him how he got there and to leave at once, or his friends would attack. Zayne saw where the man was pointing, and there stood multiple Abigors on the right side and the same amount of hydras on the left.

He stood as the sky began turning red, and there he saw the Star Witch telling him to go and tell the moon witches where he was. Trying to wake up, Zayne was so terrified. When Ladle saw him sweating and shaking, she woke him up and asked what had happened. Zayne told her the sun had taken control over the magical planet.

***

Everyone made it back to New Orleans. Amanda, for the tenth time, apologized to the siblings. She was under Danny's control, and he was against his father the whole time. Danny and Molly locked eyes as Isabel walked over to Molly and placed her hand over Molly's busted lip that was swollen from fighting with a vampire. She healed her lip and patted her shoulder.

"Danny we deserve an explanation," Isabel said.

Danny nodded. "I needed my father to believe I was on his side," Danny explained. "I left with him that day in the forest because I wanted to know where he came from and who my father was. Marcus brought me to Missouri and told me I would meet my family. That's all I have ever wanted."

Molly knew that to be true.

"In the beginning, I was on board to help him out with what he was saying, but then he talked about a stick Marcus had hidden for centuries with this older man in the year 1579. When we got there, I heard all of you. I saw Molly talking to the older man," he explained.

He told them that he was about to walk toward them, but that was when his father held him back. When he did, he knocked down a broom, and he saw Molly about to turn around when Marcus grabbed him and they disappeared. They ended up going back three weeks before that. It was Marcus's idea to warn the older man they were coming because that was when Marcus made the plan to lure all of them toward the spell. After all, Marcus wanted to bring back Damion and an evil witch his father loved. The same woman they needed for the spell.

Molly shook her head, listening to Danny's story. She told them she heard him in the back of the shop, believing what he was saying.

"That's when I knew I had to choose a side," Danny said.

"So was this voodoo witch part of the spell or just his love?" Isabel asked.

Danny shrugged. "Honestly, both, and I heard him talking about using that witch after she carried Isabel's power. She would not only bring back Damion but all his followers through the years. As for the darkness, I found out because there was a point in time when I asked why would they bring back all those people who died, and he told me for their bodies not the soul. He explained that the darkness just needs a body."

When Danny found out what killed the darkness, he knew what he had to do. Stick the magical wood from the tree his father had and place it in Damion's heart.

"We understand what you did, and it was brave to act like you were on his side the whole time to then go against his demands and help us erase the darkness for good," Isabel said.

"I actually did it for my father. The book that I found that told me how to get rid of Damion also explained what would happen to my father when the darkness was gone. How he would end his eternal life and move on in a peaceful, loving world," Danny said.

"I think that's amazing, but how did you travel back? Isn't that for witches?" Austin asked.

"That same book, actually," Danny said.

Everyone looked at each other as Tessa asked him
where the book was. Danny shrugged and told them when Marcus saw it, he took it from him. That was when his father saw how to bring Mollie Crenshaw back through the healer. It was all in that book.

Yara and Anibel looked at each other as Anibel asked him where he had found the book. Danny told them that one morning when waking up to his father sucking blood from an animal. It was a bird that he was focused on. He was drawn to the bird, and he didn't know why. The bird was sitting on the book, and as people walked by, no one saw what Danny did. The bird looked right into Danny's eyes and flew away. The book sat there as no one was paying any attention to him or the book as if they were invisible. That was the night he saw how to get rid of the darkness.

"One book tells you how to do that, and that very book also tells your father the spell to resurrect Mollie?" Hui questioned suspiciously.

"So convenient that one book helped all of your needs even if it contradicted each other," Rene said.

Everyone was silent and just thinking.

Isabel didn't have to say a word as everyone thought the same thing. This mysterious book was given to him, Yara, and Anibel, and it all sounded like the Sun Witch was part of it all. Their decisions and the spells they'd made all came from that very mysterious book. That was what Austin and Anibel were hearing in everyone's mind.

Elana spoke first, as everyone else was thinking. She told them that she was sorry, but she might have come across the book as well. Everyone looked at her. Graham knew she was hiding something.

"Okay, look, I might have known or at least guessed who my grandmother's biological family really was. I just knew in my bones that it was true about being related to all of you," Elana explained. "When I figured this out, I was all confident I was meant for so much more than being a normal human. So when I had the chance to save the world, I took it."

"Save the world?" Lucas asked.

"I met a psychic before I met Graham. He gave me a book and told me what I had been thinking before I walked into his shop—that I was meant for so much more. He literally took the words right out of my mind. The book showed me how I could capture the devil into that crystal ball, and when I did, all the evil in the world would disappear, and I would open up the heaven dimension, and heaven would appear on Earth as the two dimensions will become one," Elana said as everyone was shaking their heads. She felt the judgment on all their faces.

She stopped talking, feeling stupid for even believing she could do something like that.

"Continue, darling. We are not judging you. We just know already who would send you that book," Tessa said.

"I'm really good at knowing when I'm being played. It's just that the book knew the future, so I thought it was real and would help me capture the evil in this world," Elana said.

"Future? How did it know the future?" Graham asked.

"Well, it stated some predictions. The psychic's death was coming for one," Elana said as everyone looked at her. "He died the day I met Graham. It said on the news he had Alzheimer's, which was hard to believe, but the book said they would say that. But he died as a sacrifice for all of humanity."

"Because that's what the book said?" Rene asked.

"Well, yeah," Elana answered.

Anthony had no doubt in his mind anymore, but a smart question didn't make sense to him.

"Why was Danny told to stab Damion in the heart, but Elana was told to capture him in the crystal ball? Wouldn't they end in the same outcome without realizing it? If this book was connected."

Rene's heart started pumping fast when she was the first to put the pieces together.

"How do we know for sure Damion died? He disappeared, correct? If this book has been stirring up trouble, then who's to say it lied about killing him?" Rene questioned.

"Shit, she's right. We don't know for a fact if he died. What if the outcome was the same?" Lucas said.

Everyone began thinking again—what if this all was connected? Suddenly, Ladle and Zayne appeared.

"Mommy!" Zayne yelled out as he grabbed onto Yara.

"Zayne? What happened?" Isabel asked, looking at them.

"Zayne, tell them what you told me," Ladle said.

Zayne squeezed Yara tight. Yara sat on one knee and held Zayne's face. She asked him what was wrong. Zayne told her as everyone listened that it was time to do the moon spell and find the Star Witch because the magical planet was moving closer to the parallel universe because the Sun Witch had taken over.

Ladle told them that the Star Witch had been battling the Sun Witch for years, and all of the moon witches needed to help before everything was destroyed because if this higher power was gone, then nothing could possibly exist.

The moon witches looked at each other, feeling as if they had been hiding from the fight, and it was up to them to stop the war with the Sun Witch and save everything.

Yara asked Zayne if he knew where the Star Witch was. Anibel smiled and knew precisely what Zayne was going to say. He told everyone that they all knew where the Star Witch was. It was in their memory that was just placed away with a simple spell.

Zayne asked where a piece of paper was and a pencil. When Lucas handed it to him, Zayne began writing out the moon spell that he had been dreaming about for years. Zayne knew where the Star Witch was. It was inside a single memory in each of the moon witches, and the spell that would bring it back was in the hands of a child.

~ 14 ~

THE STAR WITCH

When the world began, it started with a single river created by two streams, one hot and the other cold. The higher you went, the streams blended together and produced a soothing sound. That river was located south of the Philippines, an island of Mindanao called Lake Sebu. Theodore was the god of the water, and he was the first creation the witches made to take over the world's waters.

As the universe grew, more and more rivers and oceans were made. The witches had a single animal that they were connected to, called a spirit animal.

The animal was given to them always to stay connected to each other. The animals were musicians like everything else. They played music with different sounds from each of the vibrations inside of them. When the Earth was made, the Star Witch had a single bird as her spirit animal. She told her bird to go and find land where each consciousness would live inside a body.

When the bird came back, he had a small piece of earth in his beak. It told the witch the Earth was ready to carry more life. That's when the three witches, Sun, Moon, and Star, spread out the magic beyond the river into the land. Each consciousness was spread out as the world grew into planet Earth.

As time went on and the universe grew, the Crescent Moon Witches spread out the gods they had created for every element throughout the universe.

As they turned into a human body, the three witches were separated, all parallel to each other. A single world was the only place they could come together
because that was the world that carried the magic inside of it. When every human became a universal entity known as a witch, the planet's magic would grow and become Larslnazm.

The entire universe will become one world seen, heard, and felt through the mind. The three parallel universes had created a multiverse as everything kept expanding. The secret of the universe is that it does end.

The magical planet could only reach so far as the universe had an ending and would begin another. It was at the end of the last creation with nothing, not a single energy or star.

When everything became one world known as Larslnazm, the three witches would continue their journey into the nothing and appear as light all over again to collide with a world of consciousness and begin their journey once again. Why was it everlasting? What was the point of continuing the journey if the three witches made a magical world when humans became witches yet had to leave it over and over?

Those answers were within the Star Witch as her story would help understand why everyone was here, and the answers to life were all in the witch's mind. The Star Witch came with the other two and could also be turned into more than one soul. Yet, she never spread into other bodies. Instead, it was an animal, and she did that because of the choices she had made.

When the Star Witch was pulled into her universe parallel with the other two, she was alone and had to guide each human into a magical being all by herself. Still, it wasn't until she fell in love with the god of the oceans that she decided to place the souls in the animals.

It began when the gods were sent throughout the universe because the Crescent Moon Witches could not only change their universe but had the power to change others. The Star Witch was upset; every change the moon witches made within the universe also happened to hers.

That caused anger between the witches. The Star Witch moved on from the anger when she found love and lived with her choice to be with her love as the Sun Witch did not. Instead, the Sun Witch grew to hate and envy the moon witches and did everything she could to become stronger than them.

The Sun Witch asked the star to join her. Still, when the Star Witch refused, the Sun Witch retaliated and used her creatures to erase the moon witches' memories because if they didn't know who they were and their universe didn't grow its magic, the sun could then expand her power and completely wipe out the moon.

If that happened, the power inside the moon would fade and eventually go out, but that kind of power couldn't just disappear. It was too powerful. Instead, it would be given to the sun because the star's power would weaken without the moon. The sun would be all-powerful and shining bright night and day.

The Star Witch wasn't angry anymore. Instead, she left her Earth and went to Kepler in her universe to be with her love, Theodore, god of the waters. She left her Earth and all of her responsibilities to be with her love. Love was a powerful feeling. It could quickly turn blissful or dreadful as an obsession could be mistaken for love, yet obsession was made from love.

The love they had wasn't blissful. It grew into something dark as Theodore fell into an obsession with the Star Witch, and that was the moment the Star Witch felt as though someone had turned him into a monster. A man chose what he did and was entirely at fault for his choices, but in this story, the Star Witch was right. Someone changed love into an obsession, and she knew only one person who was angry with her for not choosing to go after the moon witch. That same person had the ability to change love into hate and hate into love.

The Star Witch knew who used their ability to cause hate from the love Theodore had for her and created a dangerous obsession.

The Star Witch tried to leave Kepler but met a time lord who erased memories in her mind, and his name was Abigor. The minute he was killed she got her memories back. That was the beginning of her trying to reach the moon witches and warn them of the Sun Witches' retaliation. The Sun Witch was angry and wanted power from the moon witches, but what was the difference between the three of them?

The healer was the only known ability created from the moon power only. The Star Witch had no choice but to try and reach the moon witches and help them find their memories because she could not defeat the Sun Witch alone.

Her name was June, and she was the Star Witch. Her beloved animals that lived in the forest were a part of her as she spread her power and soul into the animals. When June left her Earth to be with Theodore, her animals stayed behind except her spirit animal—a bird that followed her wherever she went.

She used the bird to help communicate with the animals. She needed to leave Kepler but found herself trapped. June spent months trying to reach the moon witches while she waited for her bird to return.

One day, June was with the fairies, and all of a sudden, she heard a woman screaming. She looked around and couldn't see anything. She asked the fairies where the sound was coming from, but they didn't hear anything. June started to see flashes right before her eyes of a baby being born.

The flashes would come and go, and each time was a different moment of the baby. First, he was being born, and then she watched him grow as the next flash was a toddler trying to walk. Then she watched as the next flash was the boy standing there, yelling in an echo if anyone could hear him. She saw him staring right at her. She asked the fairies who he was. The fairies all looked at each other and shrugged. They couldn't see what June was seeing.

The boy, in another flash, was a year older and again looked at June, and when he did, she heard him talking to someone else. June looked around and wondered who he was talking to, and asked him if he could hear her. The boy said yes and asked for the Sun Witch to stop scaring him.

As soon as she heard him speak the name sun witch, she knew he had to be the connection. If he could connect with them, he had to be able to connect with the moon witch. She told him the moon witch had to find her, and she needed his help. The boy disappeared and reappeared hours later. She sat up as she waited for him to return, but just when she told him to stay away from the Sun Witch, Theodore yelled her name.

The fairies told her to come back the following morning when he was asleep because the queen of the fairies had spoken, and she said if there was a connection to the moon witches, then there might be something she could bring to them to help remind them who they are. The queen of the fairies was a very wise fairie who knew just about everything. She had met many creatures in her life and heard many stories. Everyone on this planet sought advice from the queen.

Theodore started getting louder as June nodded and ran toward the ocean. That night, she felt a sense of hope, and even though her love had turned into a monster who would not give her freedom, she went to bed smiling. June was a very strong witch, but without her animals, her power was limited. The very next morning, she woke up before Theodore and ran as quietly as she could toward the fairy tree. They were already chanting for her to come because the queen knew precisely what she should do.

June ran toward the fairies, and they flew right above her head to show her the queen's home. It was a little wooden house built in the roots of the most enormous tree and rocks in the forest. The red wooden door had a sunflower painted on it. It was a simple home with the name of the queen built over the top of her door. Her name was Alice, and she knew the secrets to the forest. The fairies told June to come inside, but she looked at the home and told them she was way too big. The fairies giggled and explained to her she was the Star Witch, and even without her animals, she was very strong in power.

June knew who she was, but Theodore had put a bracelet on her, and with that bracelet, she couldn't use her star power. The fairies knew what she was wearing, but she didn't need the star power to get inside. She just needed her mind.

The way to get inside the queen of the fairies' home was through the mind of a witch. They ordered her to sit and simply meditate. If she could get into the state of Sadhana, she would quickly appear inside. June was one of the most powerful witches. All she had to do was sit and breathe, and within minutes, her mind lifted up. She was inside the home of the queen.

One fairy told her to open her eyes, and when she did, June saw the inside of the house, yet it wasn't simple and small like the outside. It was gigantic and magical. A river was inside of the home. When June went to touch the water, she felt a sense of comfort.

She felt like she had been there before. The beautiful queen flew out, glowing head to toe. She asked June if the river looked familiar. June knew it did; she watched as the river had no ending. It simply looked as if her home went on for miles.

"How did you get such a wonderful river inside this home? One that goes beyond what we could see," June asked.

The queen laughed and wondered what happened to the Star Witch because she should know how magic works. She saw the bracelet on her and looked so sad as she flew closer.

"Oh dear, not only are the moon witches in trouble but so are you. Something is very wrong; I can feel it. We have to send this blood to one of the moon witches and get that bracelet off of you. Something happened that wasn't supposed to, and I feel as if it has to do with the magical trees because a darkness was made from the magic of the tree, and it didn't happen here, so it must have been from the moon witches," the queen said.

"Why would they make a darkness?" June asked.

"Oh, no, dear, it wasn't them. You know who it came from. That bracelet is blocking the Star Witch power from you, and the only thing that has that kind of power against your magic is you, the sun, or the moon. The moon witches lost their memories because of the same kind of power. That leaves one witch left," the queen said.

"Theodore gave it to me, and I can't get it off," June cried. She knew the Sun Witch had to be behind it.

The queen told June the river wasn't really there. It was a replica of the real one. It was the first river ever created. June looked at the river and knew it looked familiar even in its touch. She asked if it was Lake Sebu. The queen of the fairies smiled and told June that the river's power would help.

"When the boy returns, you will be ready," the queen said.

"Ready?" June asked.

"You just need to connect with the moon witches, and the boy is the answer. You will also need something the river can give you."

"And what's that?"

"Ever hear the rivers sing? They share secrets, but listening and hearing are two very different things, the queen said. "Put your hand beneath the water. Now that we have a connection, we can begin."

June looked around as all the fairies were nodding.

She reached inside the river with her hand and felt something beneath the water. She looked up at the queen of the fairies and asked if she had it. The queen smiled and told her to lift it up, and as June did exactly that, her hand began to glow.

"What is this? It looks like the plants from where I lived. Wildflowers and Moss," June said as she began to see her home right before her eyes.

The region where she lived was full of mountains and forests. Everything made a sound, and she hadn't heard that sound since she left her village. It was music to her ears. The river, birds, and wind was an instrument all on their own.

June heard a beautiful song from the Earth, and it made her want to open her mouth and sing. June controlled the vibrations of the world, and that was her ability. Her voice changed every vibration to peace and harmony. The world sang with her voice, and everything could speak through June and her songs.

She forgot she could sing as it seemed to be sleeping inside of her. She began to combine the two plants and rub it on her face and chest. June began not just to listen to the river but to hear it completely.

It sounded different than before. It was chanting a song that June felt the need to hear. It was the sound of the land, and when she sang with the Earth, she saw her birds fly right next to her.

That was when the boy appeared, and June was again in the home of the fairie. She quickly gave the blood to him. Even though her hands did not touch his, the bottle disappeared, and the boy held it in his hands. June told the boy to give it to the moon witches because they had to remember who they were and come find her because he knew where she was. The boy nodded and disappeared. When he did, the bracelet fell right off of June, and the red on the bracelet turned black.

June thanked the queen for helping her, but how did she know to give blood to them? She wondered, but only for a brief second before she realized the bracelet affected her memories because she was the one who told the fairies the hydra was her creation stolen by the Sun Witch.

June remembered everything, but with that bracelet, her mind was foggy, and her star power didn't work. She saw her bird land on her shoulder because she must have brought him back when she was in her land for that brief moment. She wanted to go back and get her other animals. That was when she was pulled outside of the queen's home and dragged down the forest.

All the fairies screamed when they saw June being dragged away by her hair. Theodore made the sea creatures find her and bring her home by her hair. The queen yelled out she had all of her power and memories back. It would just take some time to process. She had to fight now.

Everything happened so fast, but as she was getting pulled, she began to see in slow motion all her animals were walking toward them. She realized when the bird came back so did the animals.

June started to sing, and the animals with the star power used their abilities, and all of them fought off the sea creatures and the bear with the ability of super strength threw them all far, far away from where they were.

She sat up and fixed her hair and shirt. The animals all stood around her. She realized she had prepared the queen before the bracelet and told her when the boy came, she had to find the river and be reminded of the secrets of nature she once shared with the queen.

She walked her way back, meeting up with the queen once again.

"Do you now remember what else you told me to keep until this very moment?" the queen asked.

June smiled. "My dress."

She always knew the boy was coming; she just didn't know when and prepared the queen for that moment.

"Bring the dress," the queen told the fairies with a smile on her face.

All the fairies lifted a beautiful dress from inside the queen's home. It was a colorful dress with many pearls attached. The fairies placed it on June as it showed her external beauty but her interior beauty too. Her dress creates her aura. Wearing the dress, she began to make her instrument using bamboo trees.

She cut the bark for the strings and began to sing
using her instrument. The animals stood behind June as she sang a beautiful melody. The planet sang as the same vibration was heard, and it created peace and harmony. The fairies were all dancing as the music was beautiful, but one fairie interrupted

and told them to look. When the music stopped playing, everyone looked as June turned around to see.

Theodore stood there. The fairies were hesitant about what to think or do. But without saying a word, June felt the love and knew he was back.

She and Theodore danced and sang all night as the fairies joined in. The planet was finally out of the Sun Witch's commands. All thanks to the connection she had lost.

Everything seemed beautiful. She knew the moon witches were coming closer. It wasn't until days later that June saw the boy again, but this time, he was standing on a mountain and appeared scared when looking down.

June saw in a flash that Abigors and Hydras were getting ready to come after the boy. She yelled for him to go as the Sun Witch knew the moon witches had found each other, and they were ready to remember everything the Sun Witch tried taking away.

"Go, sweet boy! Tell the moon witches where you are and tell them the Sun Witch has been trying to take over our minds! I remember now because of you, and soon they will too!" she yelled for the boy to go now. He nodded and vanished.

Now, the magical planet was all she had to take control of them, and that was what she would do. The Star Witch was not held down anymore. She made her way back to Earth, and she gathered all the animals with her power inside them. She began to set up a spell, but it wasn't like all the others. It was a star spell that guided her to the planet that carried the universe's magic inside.

The Star Witch knew the humans of her universe needed her, yet she had been gone. While she was trapped, the Sun Witch stole the creature that was supposed to help the humans. Its blood could create wishes that could be fulfilled, but the Sun Witch used it to go after the moon power.

June used her power stepped inside the planet of magic and called out to the Sun Witch.
***

The moon witches gathered around and began the spell. Darkness wasn't supposed to have been made as Damion wasn't supposed to pick up that stick. Not only had it affected their world, but it also reached each parallel universe.

The moon witches held hands and knew they would take back their memories and stand face to face with the other two witches because evil lay in the darkness. It shouldn't have been able to exist in their universe. They had the power to change the timeline and erase it all from happening, and that was what they had to do. Peace was what a human had to feel to become witches as their minds would grow and become invincible to all that lay in evil.

~ 15 ~

UNDERSTANDING

Everyone gathered around the moon witches when Zayne handed Yara the moon spell. They had been doing this spell in every life. They had to find the Star Witch and erase a part of a critical timeline known for its origin of the darkness. That was not all they planned to do because this would keep happening when they were reborn. It was therefore imperative that they stopped the Sun Witch before this life was over, otherwise, their memories would disappear once again.

The difference in this life that could change everything? The child that connected them all.

The answers that lay in all of the witches would guide humans into an understanding because every human wanted to know the answers to life's questions. The Earth was telling them every day in every moment in time. The problem was they couldn't hear the sounds of the trees or the sounds of the mountains.

The sun, moon, and star placed their magic inside a planet that no one could find except the highest of power. Every time a human became a higher entity, its power would be created, and a single tree would appear on the planet of pure magic. With each tree that grew, the planet would expand more extensively and more prominently until every human became a powerful higher consciousness.

Then and only then could the planet of magic become their universe. When the spell was complete, the other moon phases' power shifted inside the healer because she would hold the power until they were reborn again.

The witches grabbed on as their friends and family stood behind them. Graham was next to Amanda, Finn, and Ladle. Danny was there holding Angela's shoulder. She was happy he was back. Blair and Doug were next to Julie. Salman and Chava were in the back with some of their followers to witness the magic. Angela looked back at Salman, and he smiled at her. Elana was standing next to Bobby and the witches of New Orleans. Just when Rene and Anthony's coven came, the moon witches began.

Almost as bright as the moon, their markings appeared to glow. The moon witches had sparkles all over them, whispering words engraved in their heads. It wasn't English, and no one around them knew what language it was, not even the other witches.

Suddenly, everyone from the moon witches' memories appeared transparent in the circle one by one; every individual in the minds of the moon witches appeared for a brief second.

It looked like movie clips going full speed inside the circle of the moon witches. Each of them was seen—Brenda, Jess, Max,

Ryan, Lyla, Annette, Clara, and many more. Then, the wind became more robust, and the trees started shaking.

The torch appeared in the sky first as everyone looked up. Along came Rosary. The wind only grew stronger as the rest of the elements were seen. Ariela, Joshua, and Maya appeared. The moon began to show a tunnel inside. Ladle pointed to the moon as everyone looked. A rainbow burst out of the moon and into each moon witch. Just as it did, the elements turned to light and flew inside the Crescent Moon Witches. When the moon closed its tunnel, the new moon witch fell to the ground, and a colorful smoke came out of her head and into Isabel's as all her doppelganger bodies appeared and also fell to the ground as their colorful smoke flew into Isabel's mind. Then came the others. The Quarter Moon Witches fell, and again, the power went into Isabel.

The gibbous all fell at the same time. The full moon witches were next. Both Anibel and her sister held hands and fell to the ground as their hands stayed holding each other. Their bodies shriveled up as time accelerated upon them.

When all of the moon power lay inside Isabel, she burst with light, and the Cresent Moon Witch's memories returned. They remembered everything—all their lives and the beginning of time. They remembered where they were from, and they knew how the world would end. They were aware that if the world didn't gain its magic and the universe didn't become one world called Larslnazm then this world would be incinerated by the sun. It would heat up and increase its rate of nuclear fusion, eventually outputting so much energy that the Earth's oceans would boil. As time went on, each planet would feel its heat, and this universe would end. That was exactly what the Sun Witch had planned.

The Crescent Moon Witches carried the healer that could overpower the Sun Witch. They were meant to save the humans and create a world of magic. They all opened their eyes as they felt more powerful than ever before.

Nathaniel appeared, holding his hand out to Zayne. He told him he was welcomed in the land that never grows, and in that land, their parents were forever inside, just as they remembered. Zayne smiled and walked toward Nathaniel, the other child made from a moon witch.

They looked at each other as their veins glowed, and they felt the energy inside of them. When everything seemed to be back to normal, Ladle walked over to her children, wondering if they still carried their personalities. Anthony hugged Ladle as every one of her children joined in except for Molly. She rolled her eyes as Austin pulled her in for the hug. Ladle wasn't mad at Molly for not wanting to hug her. Instead, she cried with happiness that Molly was still Molly.

Ladle cried, hugging her children as everyone cheered and hugged each other. Finn walked over to Rene as Ladle let go of her children and hugged Blair. Rene and Finn held each other. Rene knew he was her soulmate. When her soul was created, a piece of its energy came out and became another soul. That creation was due to magic, so when two soulmates found each other, magic would be created to take the universe one step closer to the magical world of Larslnazm.

Julie walked over and hugged Ladle next. She told Blair to tell Rene what she had found out. Blair smiled at Rene and told her the hydra was made for good, not evil, as it protected the humans and gave them wishes. Each wish could, in fact, be taken back, and Blair had found out how. Rene and Julie looked at each other and smiled. Rene knew that Blair had found a way to take back her wish, and so she would able to see Max again.

She smiled as Finn held her hand. She told Blair "Thank you," and she would reverse the spell. Blair gave Austin back his potion because she didn't need it anymore. Austin hugged Blair and told her he didn't need it either.

He walked over to Amanda and gave her the potion. Amanda was surprised and asked why he would give her such a magical potion. Austin looked at Graham, then back at her. She saw who he looked at now, knowing it had to do with her parents. Austin told her to make peace with Graham because her parents and his father shouldn't ruin both of their lives.

Amanda thanked Austin, holding the potion close to her face. She didn't want to change the past because it made her who she was today. She knew that the Crescent Moon Witches would save his father, and she didn't think she would need the potion to make peace with Graham.

Amanda hugged Austin. He knew exactly what Amanda would use the potion for, yet he didn't say a word. Instead, he just held her because she really needed a hug.

Corbin walked over to Anthony and hugged him as everyone else was hugging and overall happy the siblings had their memories back. Corbin asked what was going to happen next.

"Well, first we are bringing back Sef and saving him from being enslaved on that planet. Then, we will face the star and Sun Witches and stop this battle between us all," Anthony said. "If conscious life spreads out from the big bang and evolves on each planet even just ten percent longer, then it wouldn't evolve at all. The Sun Witch will cause destruction, and that is why we have to take our magic back and continue to help save the humans and help them use all of their five senses on magic."

"Dude, I have no idea what you just said. But cool, I'm glad you remember all that, and I will help every step of the way," Corbin said. Anthony laughed.

Beyron walked over to Molly, feeling useless that he couldn't help her through it all. They kissed, and when they did, all the Crescent Moon Witches felt magic in the air. They all took a deep breath in and slowly let it out. It was a feeling of magic from the kiss of two soulmates that only the witches could feel.

The feeling was beautiful, but then Isabel started to breathe heavily. Everyone looked at her as Anthony ran just in time for her to fall. He held her in his arms as Ladle cried, "What happened?"

The siblings looked at each other and felt it, too. Isabel just felt it stronger. Just as Rene was about to speak, night turned to day.

Everyone looked up, but their eyes couldn't completely open because of how bright the sun was. Molly saw Beyron holding his head as his eyes looked different from Molly's.

"Guys, I think the Sun Witch is here," Molly said, looking at Beyron change from love to evil. His pupils grew so large the white in his eyeballs disappeared. His skin appeared to be turning muscular as vains spread out all over. His face was filled with murderous intent.

Rene held onto Anthony as he carried Isabel in his arms. The other siblings grabbed on as the love for their family and friends became deadly. Blair started to hold her head as Salmon screamed in agony.

Love was becoming something else, and the feeling inside of them ached with pain that began in their head and gradually targeted the heart. The siblings knew what they had to do. They closed their eyes and began to turn into stardust that rose in the wind. They were carried upward into the sky and moved slowly toward space and beyond.

The siblings carried the complete moon power inside of them. They began to rise above, and as they moved through the stars and galaxies, the magic planet appeared visible again. The siblings landed on the mountain, and as they did, the dust turned into their human bodies once again. The siblings looked down at the trees, knowing they created this land.

They saw a disfigured man and realized that it was Graham's father, the Sef who was stuck there years ago, and behind him were other disfigured people. The siblings looked at each other and knew it was the other men and women that came from the sun and star universes. They had all come together on this very planet. The siblings raised their hands as the creatures began to be lifted up. They all screamed to be put down at once, threatening the moon witches.

Isabel woke up, and with her help, the creatures turned back into themselves and were scared of where they were because they didn't remember what had happened to them. The moon witches burst with magic and sent them all back to their home planets exactly where they left.

Just as the people disappeared from the magical planet, the stars in the sky grew and began to all explode above their heads, yet nothing touched the planet. As the siblings looked up at the exploding stars, animals began to walk toward them.

They all looked at the animals and were not frightened. Instead, they ran toward them. Animals followed their lead. Just as they came close enough, the animals moved out of the way, and there stood the Star Witch. The siblings smiled as they remembered who she was. They pet the animals and hugged June, but just as they were coming together, they saw Abigor standing just feet away from them.

"Oh, great. Not again," Anthony said.

"Shit. Look, now there's more," Rene pointed out.

Abigor had an army of himself behind him.

The Star Witch told the siblings the sun had been in control the whole time because she couldn't stand the thought of the moon being more vital.

"There is one more witch that you all have. The lunar witch," June said, watching the Abigors coming closer.

Isabel closed her eyes, and throughout the galaxies, an aura of light came down, and just as Isabel opened her eyes, the ball turned into a man. He was saved from the darkness and grew faster as time on his planet was different than theirs. Isabel knew where he was without thinking twice about it.

With the power of the complete moon and Star Witches, the sun had no choice but to show herself. The sun appeared as two bodies but quickly became one witch. She stared at all the other witches with an evil presence living in her eyes as if Damion was only a puppet to a much higher darkness. He was used to put her evil inside the moon witches' universe.

Damion was able to create the darkness through the magic in the tree, but it wasn't something he made like everyone thought. As soon as the Earth shifted, the darkness was brought over, and Damion felt the vibrations coming from the doors to the parallel universe that only opened as the Earth shifted. The very universe in which the Sun Witch resided.

"How do we defeat her? We don't want to kill anyone!" Austin yelled out as the creatures were getting closer.

"No, we will always need the Sun Witch, as it's meant to be the three of us," June said.

"Three? Well, I'd say four," Molly said as she pointed to the lunar witch.

"The moon has many phases, and each phase has a power of its own. The lunar witch is no exception. He is made from the power of the healer," Anthony explained.

Just then, Isabel's memories sorted out. She thought about the beginning of time when the light of the moon became a human body. Her name was Hecate, and she was just as strong as the sun and star power, but then the moon power grew.

Hecate's eyes turned into a bright blue light; she was growing in power. That was what the Sun Witch couldn't stand. Her power in one body was too strong, so she released her power to another human body, and when the moon changed phases, Hecate and the other witch she created did a spell under the full moon, quarter, gibbous, and new moon.

When they did their spell for each, gods were created, and the power of the moon spread out around the Earth to guide the consciousness into humans and begin their journey.

Isabel knew she carried the rest of the moon's power inside of her, and she would be untouchable with the lunar power. June explained that the healer was the one that carried all of the phases' power. Without the healer, the moon witch wouldn't be more powerful than the sun. She warned Isabel the Sun Witch wanted her dead.

"Don't listen to her," the Sun Witch said as she spoke for the first time. "That is not true. In fact, I know how the healer can grow into the sun instead of the moon."

June yelled out, "Liar! That's impossible!"

"You're pathetic if you don't know already that I can make the impossible possible. You were still missing one more person who has found one of my books," the Sun Witch said.

It was eye-to-eye among everyone.

"You all thought you stopped everyone from completing the spells in those books but you all don't realize I've been the strongest for years because you all lost your memories!" the Sun Witch said, smiling. "A boy who left with a broken heart didn't go home as you might have thought," she said, looking at Isabel.

They looked at each other, confused, wondering what she meant. The Sun Witch raised her hands, and everyone watched as if they were teleported somewhere else.

"Hello, Beautiful," Ryan said.

They all watched Isabel and Ryan in the middle of the street.

Isabel's eyes opened wide; she told everyone this was when she broke up with Ryan.

"Don't. I don't want to hear it. Are you breaking up with me?" Ryan asked.

Isabel couldn't bear to look. Rene put her hands on Isabel's shoulder. Isabel felt terrible for Ryan as everyone watched her walk away from him. That wasn't the only thing they came to watch. They saw Ryan walk toward the trees with tears in his eyes. Isabel didn't want to watch. She turned around as everyone gasped in disbelief. Isabel was curious and turned back around. She and everyone else watched as Ryan found a book. Isabel yelled out, "No!"

He couldn't hear or see them because they weren't really there. Their minds were flooded with the events after Isabel walked away, as the Sun Witch showed them.

Ryan opened the book, and there was a spell for making a soulmate. It allowed someone to choose who they wanted it to be, even if the universe didn't agree. Ryan took the book and left. Everyone watched him walk away with the book. The Sun Witch
appeared in closer in front of them.

"It says the real soulmate would disappear, and he will become the new soulmate of the one he chose," she said, laughing. "And he was so heartbroken, he went with it!"

They all watched Ryan do the spell, and he made the real one go away. Isabel knew her soulmate was gone, but she had no idea Ryan had something to do with it.

"You used Ryan to capture my soulmate? Why?" Isabel asked.

The Sun Witch laughed.

"Where is he?" Rene asked.

"Why are you doing this?" Isabel yelled out.

The Sun Witch shared with everyone who her soulmate was.

"Because I needed his ability to use against you of course. I need you on my side," she answered.

She explained he had an ability for hypnosis, and with a bit of time travel, he was determined to take back what Ryan tried to steal from him.

"Now that I have him, he wants his soulmate back, but not as the moon witch but instead the sun! He plans to go back and change everything so Isabel won't find her moon power. Instead, she will become a Sun Witch."

"How can he do that?" June mumbled.

The Sun Witch called out his name and told them he would bring Isabel straight to her. Just as everyone was listening to her plans, Isabel fell to the ground and was sound asleep.

***

When she awoke, she found herself in her room. That was when everything started over, but not from the beginning of time. Instead, just a year before. That was all the sun needed. Isabel's true soulmate would find her, and instead of walking toward the moon power, he would guide her the wrong way.

She was just an ordinary girl, living like everyone else—eating, sleeping, and going to school—but what felt different was her mind.

It felt as if she was suffocating in other people's feelings and emotions. Everyone seemed as if they were happy and what everyone defined as normal, but when they came in close contact with her. She felt their pain as if it was more powerful than her own.

~ 16 ~

DO-OVER

The last thing Rene heard was Isabel's shrill scream as she faded from sight.

"Where is she? Tell me right now or I swear!" Anthony yelled out, clenching his hands into fist. An evil laugh emanated from the Sun Witch. A man came out from the shadows and took next to the Sun Witch.

"This is Elijah, and he is Isabel's true soulmate."

The siblings looked at his face and saw red in his eyes, knowing he had something controlling him.

"I can't do it," Austin said as he was trying over and over to get inside Elijah's mind.

"Me either." Molly agreed because her traveling wouldn't work as well.

The siblings did not know what to do without Isabel;

they felt different.

"You better hurry because if Isabel changes at least one thing, it will affect everything, and if she follows Elijah, then all Isabel's power will be mine," the Sun Witch said, laughing.

The siblings stood in a panic as they thought about what to do. Elijah faded away, and Anthony ran toward the Sun Witch with anger in his eyes as she disappeared.

"How can she take hold of our power!" Rene panicked.

"It's the healer," June said.

"Yeah, yeah, yeah. Without the healer, we're in trouble. Ever see that *Brady Bunch* episode? 'Marsha, Marsha, Marsha?' Well, Isabel, Isabel, Isabel," Molly said. "Our power is literally away again, even after all of this!" Molly screamed at the top of her lungs, trying to travel.

"She knew Isabel was the key to your power; otherwise she couldn't defeat you all," June said.

Anthony was furious, holding his hands in fists. Rene thought about it and asked how the Sun Witch knew what went on in their universe if she couldn't come inside.

Everyone looked at each other while June thought about it. She told them the only way the Sun Witch knows exactly what goes on was if someone or something told her because the planet they were on was their only connection to each other.

Rene corrected her and told them that there were openings all around the planets and when the Earth shifted, those openings did, in fact, open as they all had seen one before.

"I gave a moon witch the hydra's blood to open portals. If it wasn't for the blood, the portals might not have been there," June explained.

"No, the Sun Witch knew about the portals and knew exactly when it was opening. The only way she keeps getting what she wants is through her mysterious books. Everyone believes they are getting what they're searching for, but instead, she is using them to get exactly what she needs," Rene said.

"So what are you thinking? How did she find out about the portals, and who do you think is helping her?" Molly asked.

"She has another book. One that was right near the mountain, so whoever saw the openings can help her understand it," Rene said.

"So we find out if there was another book by the mountain the day of the opening?" Austin asked.

"We already know who found a book by that damn mountain," Molly answered.

"Yep, Salman and Chava," Rene said.

Molly started to laugh sarcastically; she couldn't believe they were being spied on, and the Sun Witch had been using those openings to put her books into the hands of people in their universe. With her spells, she had gotten everything she wanted, and now she had Isabel in the palm of her hands.

"No, she doesn't have her yet. Isabel would have to change something, so we need to think of a way to save her," Anthony said.

"Isabel didn't know she was a witch around the time she met Ryan. Who knows what she changes," Austin said.

Anthony had an idea. "Yes, Isabel is needed for our abilities, but we are still the moon witches. We still have power, and if we just need more magic, we will call upon the angel again."

"Wait, I know we have trusted her and put the keys in her hands to help us find our planet, but the book Danny used guided Marcus to the angel. If it was the Sun Witch's spells that Danny used, then did Marcus go to the heaven dimension?" Rene questioned.

Everyone was silent. "We were in a trance, but we felt her there," Molly said.

"But you guys never really saw her there?" June asked.

Everyone was silent again, thinking.

"Don't fucking tell me!" Molly yelled out. "Why do we keep falling for her tricks?"

When they were holding hands and in a spell, they

couldn't see Marcus leave. The siblings looked at each other, thinking they just heard what had happened from everyone around them, and they didn't see her for themselves.

"One way to find out. We are going to the heaven dimension," Anthony said.

***

September 2021, The first day of autumn and the day Isabel found out she was a witch. She was late for school and felt like something was off, but she didn't know what. She shook her head to snap out of it and ran to school because the entire day seemed off when she was late for something.

Isabel made it to school just as the bell rang, and when she ran to the school door, she heard her name. She turned around and didn't walk into the building where Ryan would have been standing.

Instead, she turned around while he shut the school door. She looked around to see who called out to her.

"Hello? Who called me?" Isabel asked as she swore she heard her name loud and clear.

"Isabel," the voice said again.

Isabel took a step away from the door. Ryan stood in the hallway, ready to meet the one he had a connection with. Blair sent him there to meet her.

"What is it? I'm late!" Isabel yelled out as she turned around to walk toward the door again.

"It's me, Isabel. I can't let anyone see me because I'm skipping class. Come with me," Elijah said as he walked toward Isabel. He stopped when she was able to look at him, and he held out his hand and told her to come.

Isabel looked at him and couldn't believe what she saw. He was a handsome boy with a smile that made her blush, and there were butterflies in her stomach just by him looking at her the way he did. He wore a dark green army shirt that complemented his muscles so well. Isabel thought he looked like a military boy; clean shaven and very fit. Even though she's not a big fan of military boys, he sure looks like he can survive in the wilderness with nothing but a stick. She told him she didn't know who he was, so why would she just go with him?

Elijah smiled and walked closer to her. He told her if anyone saw him, he would get into trouble and asked if that was what she wanted in a flirty tone. He smiled again, and she couldn't help but smile back.

"I have the answers for why we feel different than everyone else and why their emotions feel like they're suffocating us. I thought it was just me, but there has always been some sort of attachment I feel when I walk past you," Elijah said, knowing they were truly soulmates so she was going to feel the same.

"I've never seen you before," Isabel said.

"Look." Elijah walked closer and touched her hand. Isabel felt exactly what he was talking about.

Isabel looked shocked. He told her that they could go and talk, or the school would tell them to get back to class, and they would never get a chance to find out why.

The janitor opened the door, and Elijah told her again to come just for one day, and she wouldn't regret it for a moment. Isabel looked back at the janitor who was carrying a bucket in his hand.

"Shouldn't you be in class, missy?" the Janitor asked.

Isabel ran, and she didn't think of anything else except getting away from the school. As she got further and further away, part of her wanted to stop running. But the other part had never done anything like this, and it seemed exciting.

Elijah grabbed her hand, and they ran and didn't stop until they were far, far away from the school, and Elijah knew they were away from Ryan, too.

Ryan stood there in the doorway of the school and knew he was being timed. He looked around but didn't see Isabel anywhere.

Isabel was out of breath, and the trees seemed to be blowing even though there wasn't much wind where they were standing. Isabel looked up to the trees and wondered why they were moving so much. It looked like they were telling her something, but she couldn't hear it. Isabel told Elijah that maybe this was a bad idea as she turned to walk back to the school.

"Wait. I want to show you something." Elijah held out his hand. "It's something magical."

"Magical?" Isabel asked. She couldn't help but become intrigued by Elijah. But still had her guard up. "I know how to throw a punch if you try something, ya know?"

Elijah smiled as it wasn't a smile from trying to trick her. It was a genuine smile. He didn't know why he'd done that because he was under the Sun Witch's command, but something about her made him genuinely smile. He quickly caught himself and stopped smiling. He told her he wouldn't hurt her, and he wouldn't expect anything less than her protecting herself.

"Plus, it's a public place. Calm down," Elijah said.

Isabel thought about it as she looked around. "Okay, make it quick. I shouldn't be skipping school."

He grabbed her hand as she pulled away and told him to go in front of her. He held his hands up as he agreed he would go, and she could follow. They walked and walked as one mile turned to two. Just as Isabel was about to ask how much longer, Elijah told her they were there.

She looked around and didn't see anything except stores and houses, but nothing magical. She asked where they were because she had never seen that block before. He told her they weren't in her town anymore.

"That's Impossible. I know my town. We went by the church, and then I saw the bridge. But where is the library? We are on a block I've never seen, but we didn't leave the town yet." Isabel looked around, trying to recall her memories of the town.

She turned around and looked in the distance where they walked. "I'm confused."

Elijah saw she was very lost and thinking way too hard.

"That's the magical part. We're in Tennessee, and the house in front of us was the Bell witch's home."

"What in the world are you talking about?" Isabel yelled out nervously.

Elijah pointed to the house. "We're here. This witch will explain why we feel the way we do and knows our family very well, too."

"Witches? Okay. I've played along this whole time because I do feel something when I'm with you. And how you knew about everyone's emotions affecting me so much, but witches? I'm leaving. There is no way I'm going with you inside a house with no witnesses," Isabel said.

Walking away, Elijah grabbed her hand, and when he did a flashback came to the both of them of a life they shared together. It was them in a cornfield. She was wearing a dress that blew in the wind, and he wore a suit.

He kissed her hand in the vision they both had. With a sense of longing, she kissed his lips. He grabbed her face as they shared a passionate kiss.

Hearing a voice caused the vision to fade away.

"I'm glad you both are here," a woman said as she opened her door.

"Did you see that too? Us In a cornfield?" Isabel asked. But before Elijah could answer, the woman told them to come now.

Isabel and Elijah were in a complete trance. All they could do was stare into each other's eyes.

"Elijah!" the woman yelled out.

He snapped out of it and looked at the woman. Bowing his head to her, he told Isabel to come.

Isabel didn't put up a fight. She walked toward the house as if she didn't feel scared of or threatened by Elijah after that vision. He was surprised. He thought he would have to do more to get her inside but was caught off guard when she just walked right in.

"Come with me," Isabel said before walking inside. "I'm not going without you."

Elijah smiled at her and blushed. All of a sudden, he felt the need to protect her as if the brainwashing was gone. He was about to tell her not to go inside, but the woman looked him straight in the eyes a few inches away from his face.

"That is all the Sun Witch needs from you. You better go now," she said, shutting the door behind her and Isabel.

He yelled out, "No!" Regretting everything he just did, he knew what happened, but he had no control over it. He yelled out he wanted to help, let him inside, but the Bell Witch made the doors and windows of the house disappear.

Elijah was still under the Sun Witch's command, but the connection the two souls had with each other was too strong. He didn't want to leave Isabel inside alone. He looked at the house, knowing that she was inside, and he couldn't get in. His body and mind started fighting off whatever the Sun Witch had done to him.

He wanted to help Isabel, and he told her he wouldn't hurt her. He couldn't get her smile out of his head. Elijah stood thinking about what he should do when Ryan appeared. He looked at Ryan.

"Can you see me?" Ryan asked.

"Yes, why?" Elijah asked.

"So you're a witch? Do you know where Isabel is?" Ryan asked.

Elijah hated Ryan for trying to take his place but needed someone to help get Isabel out. He told Ryan what happened, and he needed help fixing what he had caused.

"Where are her siblings? They can help," Ryan said.

"No, where we are they don't even know they're witches yet," Elijah answered.

Ryan and Elijah stood side by side in front of the house where Isabel was trapped, and they both knew they had to work together to save her.

***

Isabel saw the doors and windows disappear.

"Elijah!" she screamed. She ran toward the wall where the door would have been.

"Help me! Someone get me out of here!" Isabel yelled. She looked around, knowing she was stuck.

The Bell Witch laughed as a man and a little girl walked out carrying some tea and sugar. The man asked Isabel to sit, and he and his daughter would give her some tea. Isabel looked confused about why they were so calm and holding a cup of tea. The Bell Witch ordered them to leave as soon as they put down the tea and sugar. The man held his daughter's hand and rushed out of the room. Isabel felt their fear and knew they were trapped as well.

She played it off and sat down by the tea. She asked calmly what the witch wanted with her. The witch told her she had a deal she was willing to make with her. Isabel tried not to look nervous and asked what the deal was. The witch said to her if she drank the tea, all her power would come out, and then the two humans in the other room wouldn't die. Isabel heard the little girl breathing very heavily, and she heard the father praying to a god, holding his child.

She was left with a choice. She looked at the tea and took a deep breath as the father and child's life were in her hands. She asked what power was inside of her. The witch told her it was stolen and put inside of her, but now she had to give it to the rightful owner, the Sun Witch.

She would make sure Isabel and those two humans lived a peaceful and wonderful life.

It seemed like an easy choice for Isabel because she didn't know the power the witch was even talking about, and yet she could save those two people. When the witch told her they would live a peaceful and wonderful life, she felt the lies and deceit coming off of her.

Isabel heard the father and child weeping in the other room. The witch held up her hands, and when she did, the two humans were being choked by magic. Isabel couldn't believe what was happening as they were in separate rooms but seemed to be choked by the witch.

"Make your choice!" the Bell Witch said.

Isabel picked up the teacup, and the witch smiled and bowed her head.

"Isabel, please wait. I am coming," a voice whispered into Isabel's left ear.

"What?" Isabel said as she looked around to the left of her. "Did you hear that?"

"No! Hear what? Make your choice now!" the witch said.

Isabel knew she needed to stall. Elijah would be there soon.
***

"Well, in order to know how to defeat this witch, we need to know who she is," Ryan said.

"Yes, right," Elijah said.

"So, who is she? Hello! You are the one working with her so who the hell is she?" Ryan shouted.

"I don't know. She was sent from the Sun Witch," Elijah answered.

"Great."

"Wait, I do know the Sun Witch can only mind control people who have died but haven't gone to the other side, or the heaven dimension just yet. As soon as the spirit leaves the body, that's when the Sun Witch captures and uses them."

"That doesn't really help, man... Wait, is that what she did with you?" Ryan asked.

Elijah nodded.

"How did you get out of the mind control?" Ryan asked.

"Our connection helped. The soul connection we have."

Ryan seemed confused because he thought he was Isabel's soulmate. Elijah didn't have time to explain. He just said it didn't matter. What mattered was saving Isabel.

"You're right. So you said the witch who has Isabel is dead?"

"Yes."

"Okay. I know how to get inside. I know someone who can help. She's the one who brought me here, and she can help with spirits," Ryan explained.

Not being able to get inside the magical house, they went to Blair instead.

After they explained what had happened, Blair made it clear she couldn't deal with two witches at a time. He would have to go back and then she could bring that witch straight to her house. Ryan looked disappointed.

"So I'd have to go back? I can't meet her, can I?" Ryan said.

"I'm sorry, Ryan. Another time, maybe. But if you go back, I can channel that witch's spirit straight to me," Blair said.

"I get it. Save her. I will go back now," Ryan said.

Elijah saw the sadness in his eyes and felt like he was a good dude, but he did have a question before he left.

"Why did you take a spell that would kill someone and take their soulmate?" Elijah asked as bluntly as possible.

Ryan didn't know what he was talking about, but he knew Elijah was serious and remembered Elijah said he was killed. Ryan put the pieces together quickly.

"Just take care of her. We have no time," Ryan said. "And If I did that, I'm sorry. I feel connected to her." He disappeared.

Blair tried and tried, but the Bell Witch would not come to her. Her nose started to bleed.

"What's the matter?" Elijah said.

"It's not working. I can't reach her."

She tried again, but Elijah felt like Isabel was left with a choice that was going to kill her. He just knew they needed to do this now. "Isabel, please wait. I am coming," he mumbled to himself.

"I usually work with spirits on the other side, but since this witch hasn't made it there, it's harder than I thought." Blair had used a lot of her power and knew she had to use plan B—a young boy.

Blair picked up the phone, and before dialing a number, she told Elijah she knew someone who might be able to talk to the dead when they were still on Earth, and he could use that power to channel the angel and ask for her help. Elijah asked why she said the word "might" and didn't have time to be wrong.

She dialed the number and waited for them to pick up. As she waited, she told Elijah he was just a boy and hadn't come into his full power just yet, but he and his mother came to her shop for a psychic reading, and Blair believed he saw the dead.

When the mother and boy agreed, Blair and Elijah teleported straight there. Elijah took one look at the boy's eyes and felt like he had seen him before but didn't know where or when.

Blair thanked them for helping, but the mother explained she didn't think her son could help. But after everything Blair had done for them, she would have him try. Blair told everyone to sit and they would contact the angel. If the Sun Witch came in and took the soul, the angel would know, and she would guide them on what to do.

They all held hands in a circle of chairs. Blair looked at the boy and told him she would be by his side the whole time, and nothing would happen that would scare him. The boy nodded, and Blair began.

She closed her eyes, talking to the angel. She couldn't get into heaven, but she could use the boy's power as he repeated everything after her. Elijah saw clouds appearing in the room and a light above them. It was working.

~ 17 ~

HEAVEN

Despite seeing nothing but gray, the rest of the witches kept moving upward, feeling their bodies being pulled.

In a flash, gravity disappeared, leaving them with a strange feeling. Their bodies became light as a feather. They felt themselves float. As they floated up, any negative feelings were gone from their minds. They began to feel a sense of love.

Peace and harmony filled their minds. Suddenly, their clothes disappeared, but they couldn't see or even think of different body parts.

They all were the same in their minds, blocking out any differences in their bodies, and only saw a figure with no detail, yet they felt beauty all around.

Their hair turned gray, and their scars, scratches, or any mark the Earth had given them all disappeared.

A woman appeared with the most beautiful wings, sparkling in the light, with a blue tint that reminded them of the sky and ocean.

The siblings all looked over. The angel was happy to see them again. She had been waiting for them to come and open the planet of magic.

When she asked them about her brother, it confirmed they were right, and he wasn't with her.

"I saw what happened. My brother was taken away by what looked like me," she said. "I couldn't do anything to stop her. It's not me who can stop her. It's all of you."

"You are a loyal being and perfect to guard the heavens, but the Sun Witch is definitely someone we will deal with," Anthony said.

"The Sun Witch wants to be stronger. That's what this is all about. She has been trying to take the healer for herself because with the healer comes with phases, and with that, the power is beyond anything me or her have," June explained. "We need to find her."

The angel understood and took out her hand. She raised them up, and a single tree appeared. The branches were huge and carried the most beautiful leaves, but stones of every color were on the leaves. It was the Tree of Life and the first tree they ever made.

The tree was created from magic, and the siblings touched the tree because it felt like home. The angel told them her father was evil, but her mother came from that same tree.

As she spoke, the siblings recalled the memories.

"I remember your mother was the very first human-made as her consciousness was made from the tree of life. Your father wasn't always bad. He was forced to pick up the stick. You know that, right?" Rene asked

"Yes, I've seen him before I was born, but the evil was all I knew of him." The room was silent for a moment. "Thank you, though. I needed to hear that," the angel said, smiling at Rene. "This tree will help you change all of that and save Isabel."

She waved her hand, and right away, they all saw Isabel about to drink something that would take her power away. It would then grow in the Sun Witch.

An intense vibration suddenly erupted, and the angel told them she was being called upon. The siblings looked at June. She smiled as they all just knew who it was.

They all closed their eyes as their minds connected with a young boy, and then...as they got closer to the calling....they felt Blair.

Blair yelled out for the angel and, within seconds, saw the rest of them. She cried with happiness and asked for all of their help because Isabel was in trouble. They were all together as the crystal ball saw inside of the heaven dimension. The angel put her hand on the tree of life when the siblings and June did, too. Blair and Elijah grabbed onto the crystal ball, and the boy's nose started to bleed.

They pulled Isabel with a force of energy that only magic could create. Isabel went to sip on the tea, but just as she touched it with the top of her lip, she disappeared in the blink of an eye.

The Bell Witch screamed and grabbed the man and his daughter. Isabel appeared in heaven with her siblings, but she couldn't feel guilt or nervousness as only peace and love were inside the dimension.

Isabel couldn't help but destroy the peace because her feelings were more substantial than anyone. She started breathing heavily.

"No! She's going to hurt them! I have to!" she yelled out.

Isabel felt angry and scared as the heavens began shaking. This energy didn't belong in this dimension, but Isabel carried it strongly. Blair lost contact with them.

Rene asked what was happening as the angel began to feel scared, and she had never felt that before. She told them that the negative feelings were wiping them out.

Isabel tried to calm down, but for the first time, the Sun Witch opened the heaven dimension as it fell apart. The cracks began to glow with the sun's heat coming through.

The tree was the only thing not moving, and the angel told them to grab on, and just when they did, they saw their father. He grabbed on with them and told his children to go back and change it all. He always told his children never to change the past, but he never knew the Sun Witch had caused all of it. It was a fixed point in time that only the moon and Star Witch could undo.

He told his children they would be the only ones that would remember. They began to think about all the people involved, and Isabel didn't want Angela to forget that it was all connected to the evil that Damion brought into this universe.

James told them, knowing how they felt about it. The stones from this same tree were the ones that could hold the memories of it all, and it would be hidden in a place they would never forget. James yelled out as the heavens began to crumble. He would still be gone and wanted his children to be strong and fight for their people no matter what creature it was.

He reminded them that with a higher consciousness, the universe and all the planets would become one world, a world called Larslnazm, and that was when he would see them again.

"But if we remove everything the Sun Witch causes, why would you still be gone?" Molly asked. "You died from that darkness Damion brought over."

James knew what he was about to say would hurt his children. "The lunar moon power was turned to darkness, yes, but....." As he hesitated to finish that sentence, Anthony said the words.

"But since it was a moon power, your death will not change," Anthony said with his eyes opened wide. "The moon power is just too strong. Our power is just too strong."

"*What?* So we can change it all except his death? What the Fu—" Molly yelled out as Isabel pushed her shoulder.

Isabel glanced at where they were to show Molly that now was not the time to swear.

"If the moon power kills, the soul will not come back," James said.

That was why he couldn't be reborn, but that wasn't what he told them originally because he didn't want to hurt them. He told them he would be the arc angel of the heavens to protect the goodness and purest of their universe and help the angel collect the old souls.

When every person ran out of lives, their spirits would become balls of consciousness inside the heaven dimension, and only if that energy was one of a witch would the magic grow and be placed inside the trees on the magical planet.

James told his children he loved them and to tell Ladle he would one day see her again.

They yelled out that they loved their father, closed their eyes, and began to use the power they carried inside their minds, bodies, and souls. The tree lit up, and everything began to disappear slowly.

Standing in the forest the very moment Damion was
walking toward them. Molly saw where Damion was going and saw a very stick he would of found. She ran and picked up the stick and asked if this was it. It started to glow with Molly's touch. They knew the answer.

June told them to grab onto each other as they had to hide the tree. They said a spell, and the tree disappeared.

Hecate was walking miles away, but she looked toward the forest and knew what happened when time changed, and right in the back of her shoulder, she felt a hand. When she looked over, it was the lunar witch.

He asked her what this meant for them because he, too, knew time had changed. Hecate smiled and told him the darkness wasn't there, and the vampires and werewolves would come together because of a child that would be the hybrid and bring together the two creatures. This time, not for war but instead, from the peace the hybrid would bring when he was born.

Hecate and the Lunar Witch held hands, and soon, they spread their souls into different bodies under the moonlight. A bit of magic went into the universe as a soulmate was born and forever connected.

"It's time for us to go back to our time," June said.

"What about this stick?" Molly asked.

Everyone looked at each other, knowing Damion was going to see them. They disappeared just as Damion walked right past the spot where the stick was lying, and everything changed. Damion lived out his life as father of two. He fell in love with a woman who lived in Tennessee but moved out, and now the house was owned by the Bell family, a lovely couple with their children living a simple but happy life.

Marcus, his son, still became a vampire but fell in love with a werewolf, and their baby became history. The angel still became an angel and trustworthy for the witches. She stood side by side with James as they were put in charge of the heavens. The sun's doings all changed, but the moons power made everything happen the way it was supposed to happen.

The moon witches brought the stick with them and stood inside the planet of magic. They called out to the Sun Witch, and she appeared in front of them. The Star Witch looked at the moon witches and saw for a brief second each of them in all of their lives. Their faces were different but their crown and heart chakras lit up with the same magic light.

"You want more power. That's why you turned what would have been and twisted it with the energy of evil darkness, and it changed our path to our home. With this stick, we will be able to connect through the sun, moon, and star. This planet of magic will be put inside each of the portals. Once you place the stick inside your universe, it will keep the moon out even during the day, and the magic we all share will become us all," all of the siblings said at once.

"You are giving me part of the tree you created? But the darkness?" the Sun Witch said.

The witches held on to the stick and said the words, "Crystol anasa mi omblay. Crystol anasa mi omblay. Crystol anasa mi omblay." Their eyes lit up. "Crystol anasa mi omblay." The stick turned blue, and the siblings smiled.

"You have evil inside of you, and it will be let go into the multiverse. It will leave you some room for love and kindness, and the evil will spread evenly," June said.

"Why? Why are you doing this? Helping me yet putting evil in your universe?" the Sun Witch questioned.

"We are the creators, and we will be there when something goes wrong. Every individual in our life is born good and pure no matter what anyone believes, so when evil happens, it won't be in the form of darkness that spreads and cannot be taken out except from magic. Instead, it will be all in their minds, and they will be able to fight off their evil all by themselves. They wouldn't need magic to bring out their humanity; they just need to breathe and look up to the sun, moon, and stars to find the portal we are placing to us," Isabel explained.

The world was never going to be perfect, and that was all, of course, for a reason. Good or bad, there was a choice, and the witches wanted everyone to know that. There wasn't a place that was more evil than others. It is spread out evenly in all races, ethnicities, religions, lands, genders, and planets in the universe. All of the evil was simply in their minds.

When a human was born, they were not evil as their consciousness became human. It could be manipulated by evil, but there was a way to let go of it all. It was finding the witch inside of you. The world as they knew it evolved, and when they raised their consciousness, there would be a time when it renewed again.

Every creature on every planet had to understand and listen to their planet. On Earth, every river should be clean enough to drink. Water was sacred, just like the air.

The siblings could feel it all. They knew the answers and what they must do. They would help the humans of their universe, and with the star and Sun Witch, the evil would have no power in a world of pure witches that were guided by the moon, sun, and stars.

Molly went over and handed the Sun Witch the stick made from the Tree of Life. The same stick that would harm a moon witch but was now shining a blue light out of it, carrying a different ability.

The Sun Witch nodded her head and disappeared as anyone would wonder what she would do next. Maybe there was a chance she would try something evil, but the siblings knew she wouldn't. Instead, she brought it to the universe parallel to theirs, and when she did, the stick did exactly what the witches had said.

The evil burst out of her and spread everywhere. Where there was a universe, there was evil. The Sun Witch did feel a sense of peace, and her power of obsession disappeared, and love was the only power she carried. She could make anyone fall in love. Cupid, some would say.

The evil was on planet Earth, but the witches made sure it could be lifted from every person. If they just
opened their minds, the temptations would disappear. Once they became a universal entity, evil couldn't touch them. The higher the conscious, the closer they were to the witches. And they would protect them
from the evil. It was all in the mind, and when they could control the mind, they would be able to control everything.

~ 18 ~

THE BEGINNING OF THE END

On the chilly morning of December 5th, 2022, Angela was walking to school when Isabel, Molly, and Austin approached her. Isabel asked if she recognized them. Angela smiled and said yes, and they all had a sigh of relief, but then....Angela said they went to her school.

"But are we friends?" Isabel asked as she watched Angela look confused. "Do you remember your father and Chava? The Shasta Mountains?" Isabel was panicking.

"What about my father?" Angela asked confusedly.

"Dammit!" Isabel said, looking at Molly. "We have to get those stones."

"Where do you think it is? Father said in a place we feel connected to," Molly asked.

They all watched Angela laugh at them awkwardly and run off to school. They stood there thinking. Austin pointed to the tree in the forest, the one they used to go to as children.

"Wait. I know the moon power stays the same, and what was supposed to be wouldn't change either, but the moon power didn't cause the tree to be there. Why would that be meant to be if it was just used to escape from Abigor so—" Molly said as Isabel interrupted.

"It would also coexist with why we are still on planet Earth, now would it?" Isabel said.

Austin knew what Isabel was thinking. "We were meant to be here on planet Earth weren't we? The Sun Witch just twisted it, but no matter what, we are supposed to be here."

Isabel smiled as Molly questioned it.

"I wonder why," Molly said. "If it wasn't to escape from Abigor, then why did our mother still come here?"

Suddenly, a light shot up behind them from the tree they were connected to.

Molly ran to the tree, and as soon as she came back, she gave a ring to Isabel.

"It's all there—stones, jewelry, all of it. We have to start reminding our closest friends, and well, you're the one with the human friend," Molly said.

Isabel thanked her and took the ring to catch up to Angela.

***

The siblings remembered all the timelines, but now Angela would not forget the one that just changed as long as she was wearing the ring. Angela took a deep breath as her pupils grew and shrank within seconds. She hugged Isabel, and after Isabel explained what the ring was for, she asked her what if she has to take it off to wash her hands or something.

Isabel wasn't sure what would happen until the ring started shrinking. Angela told them it was getting tighter when suddenly it turned into a ring tattoo and the pain went away.

Molly smirked, running over to them. "Badass. Well, it's made from pure magic. Of course, it wouldn't come off."

"What about everyone else like my father?" Angela asked.

Only the people closest to them would remember, but as for everyone else. It was all supposed to be this way. Not knowing was fine, too, because soon, with the help of the witches, they would all know the truth.

Salman and Chava were first with Amanda, and the wolves were next. Amanda thanked them again as she kissed Austin on the cheek. Austin smiled and planned to come back to New Orleans again. The New Orleans witches and the vampires of Salem all wore the ring.

Just as they were leaving Salem, Finn asked the three of them where Rene was. Molly told him she was in Altair with her coven, and she and Anthony planned to graduate and become the leaders of Altair's soldiers of witches. They would fight and protect the universe, so they didn't think she would return to Earth anytime soon.

"But know, the moon witches can never stay away from Earth too long," Isabel said with a smile.

Finn smiled back, and from the corner of his eye, he saw Marcus walking toward him. Finn asked the siblings if Marcus would get the ring, too, but they looked at each other and told him no. Marcus was better off not knowing the evil he had done. Finn agreed and walked toward Marcus. He hugged him and asked if he wanted a drink. Marcus smiled and told him he would never turn down a drink.

Molly knew his wife died years ago but wanted to know if Danny was still alive or if he died too. After all, the timeline changed. Years went by, and he lived them all knowing he was the Hybrid.

Her nerves were just too strong to hear the worst possible answer right now, so she didn't ask.

The siblings went on and traveled to Clara, Dominic, and Annette. Traveling to everyone they could think of and giving them a ring. When they arrived at the space station to see Susie to give her a ring, they saw the building abandoned.

Molly told Isabel if the darkness never happened, that meant they messed up Susie's life completely. Isabel shook her head in disbelief. Their father told them their lives on Earth were as normal as before, as nothing really changed drastically. If Susie was gone, that was a highly drastic change. Molly agreed with Isabel but looked around and told Isabel she wasn't there because it looked like no one had been there for years.

Austin said maybe Molly was right. Molly gestured for them to follow because they had to find her. Austin asked, "Where should we even start?"

Their attention was drawn to the building's side by a noise. Molly, Austin, and Isabel's head turned immediately in that direction. Isabel started running toward it, calling out for Susie.

"You gotta be kidding me. Has she ever seen any horror movie in her life? Never run toward the noise," Molly said.

"Honestly, she probably hasn't. She watches those Lifetime movies when men are always the evil ones," Austin said. "But let's go. We gotta be her backup now." He walked toward Isabel.

Molly rolled her eyes and followed. They tiptoed in just as they were approaching the building's corner. The minute they turned slowly around the building, they saw a homeless lady pushing a cart. Isabel asked the lady if she was okay. They all looked toward the lady dressed in rags and a garbage bag, trying to see her face.

The lady turned around, and Isabel yelled out in excitement.

"Susie! I knew it. You're here!.."

"Do I know you?" Susie asked in a low, raspy voice.

"From the looks of it, we're here to change your life," Molly said as she looked inside the cart Susie was pushing. Garbage completely overflowing inside.

Isabel clapped her hands in excitement and told Molly to get out of the ring. Molly took it out of her pocket, and Isabel grabbed it at full speed; Molly didn't have time to react. She put the ring on Susie's dirty cut-up finger, and within a single second, Susie remembered everything.

"Wait, so I remember doing things and creating the most wonderful inventions, but I technically didn't do any of that, now did I?" Susie asked as she looked down at herself and the cart she was pushing. "I had dreams of doing all of that, but I walked a different path, one that I regret every day."

The siblings all looked at each other before they looked up at the sky.

"What are you all looking at?" Susie asked as she looked up.

Before they could answer, she saw a single star in the sky even though the sun was out bright as could be.

"Wow, that star is bright even with the sun is shining," Susie pointed out. Isabel smiled.

The star started to glow brighter and brighter. Susie squinted her eyes and asked if there was a portal inside the star. The moment Susie saw that, the siblings touched the building. It started to fix itself up and look new again.

Isabel told her she owned the building, and if the world just took a glimpse at her creations, they would know she *was* somebody. She was a scientist.

"Magic and Science," Susie said excitedly.

"Magic and Science. They just go hand in hand," Isabel replied.

Susie's clothes started changing into a white robe. She ran to the door to go inside. Noticing the siblings still standing there, she asked if they were coming with her.

"We have to go now," Austin told her. "We will definitely be back."

"Yeah, asking for help, probably." Molly laughed.

Susie gave them one last hug and told them she was going to change history.

"Do you have an invention already in mind?" Isabel asked.

"Teleportation. Scientifically, of course," she said as they all laughed, eager to see what she came up with.

The three of them held hands and wished her the best. Seconds later, they disappeared. Susie looked up at the star again and noticed it wasn't there. Then she began to feel her ring getting tighter. It was no longer a ring. It was a tattoo that could never come off.

"Wow," Susie mumbled to herself as she walked into her new building. "Magic and Science. I can work with that."
***

When the siblings returned home, they made it just in time for school. Isabel walked away, and so did Austin. Molly still couldn't get Danny out of her head. Was she going to see him at school? She thought to herself, *Probably not. He's too good for that now.*

Her thoughts kept getting faster and louder.

"You guys tell me if Danny is inside. I can't look!" Molly yelled out to Austin and Isabel.

"Why can't you look at me? Am I that much of a sexy beast?" Danny asked as he walked up behind Molly. "Pun intended. After all, I am literally a sexy gay beast." Isabel went to class with a smile on her face.

Molly and Danny hugged. She realized she didn't have to give him a ring. He was already wearing it.

"Oh, good. You have the ring. That's how you remember everything. Cool. Who gave it to you?" Molly asked.

"Oh, this? My mom did before she passed away," he said. "How do you know about this ring?"

She was about to tell him, but there, across the street, was Clara. Molly knew Clara was the one who made that happen. It was a thank you for saving the world from the Sun Witch and saving her sister Annette from a life of black magic.

Molly smiled and knew she had brought Danny back to her. After seconds of quick thinking, Danny just couldn't resist and gave Molly a wedgie.

"Let's go to class, loser, finish this year, and then travel the world," he said.

Molly laughed, walking toward the school. "That sounds perfect."

Standing next to the school doors, Danny told Molly he liked her hair. He asked if the badass girl was gone too, like the black in her hair.

Molly laughed and grabbed his hand. Instead of walking into the school, she opened the door and appeared on a winding country road.

"These kids are bullies, bro," Molly said, pointing toward the forest where a group of kids were at the same place Molly remembered from the last time she was there.

"So what do you plan on doing?" Danny asked.

"I plan on giving them a taste of their own medicine," Molly said.

"Ah, so this is about my 'are you still a badass' comment?" Danny asked, laughing.

"This is exactly about your badass comment," Molly said as she swayed her hands and mumbled some words. She used a spell and made them all pee their pants, but it wasn't just pee. It was pure diarrhea coming out the other side. As they all ran home, kids from school saw them and started laughing. Even the boy they were bullying last time had a smirk on his face because karma had hit the bullies right in their asses, literally.

***

Back at school, Austin sat in class trying to concentrate but kept thinking about how Graham was no longer around. He and Elana were a couple now and chose to live on planet Cassini. He took over the land and made homes for himself, Elana, his father, her mother, and his grandmother. They all lived side by side on the land Graham was once running from. But now it was their home, and black magic wasn't allowed.

Just rooms away, Isabel was in class, also distracted as she sat and thought to herself. She thought about how before Elana and Graham left, she was able to see Elana's grandmother, the one she met years ago but as a child, when they needed a lock of hair.

She held the grandmother's hand, and right away, the elderly lady remembered her.

"You look the same. You didn't grow up?" the grandmother asked.

"It's magic, and thank you for never being a witch hunter. You truly are the purest heart," Isabel said.

Isabel was suddenly brought out of her thoughts as Jess walked up to her.

When Jess was standing right above her desk, she glanced at Angela. Angela was staring back.

Isabel knew who Jess really was. She was one of the mean girls and didn't stand up for Isabel when she needed a friend. Even though Jess didn't remember, Isabel did. She knew that something else could happen in the future, and Jess wouldn't stand by her side. Isabel should have walked away, but she had hope that maybe Jess was different in this life. And even if she wasn't, Isabel felt sorry for her because even the popular girls would use Jess as a puppet.

Isabel smiled when Jess asked her to go out after school. To Angela's surprise, Isabel agreed. Isabel got a text message as Jess walked to her desk.

Angela: *Are you kidding me?*

Isabel: *I won't be fooled by her. I already know what kind of person she might be.*

Angela: *So why would you hang with her knowing she would most likely stab you in the back if Stacy gets a hold of her?*

Isabel: *I have changed, but thank you for caring! Don't worry. I know how to handle her. I'm not turning my back on people like her or anyone. You know who I am.*

Angela: *Yeah, smart, but right now, you're being...*

Isabel: *A leader to guide humans to magic. All humans.*

Angela: *...*

Isabel smiled, knowing Angela didn't know what to say. She looked over at her, and Angela just shrugged her shoulders when class began.

***

Ladle was at home making plans for her store because as soon as they graduated, she would be
leaving this planet for good. She'd made up her mind because she missed her home.

She sat on the floor, reading about business and everything that she had to prepare for. That was when Ladle felt a cold breeze pass her by. She got up to shut the window and felt another breeze. When she turned around, she saw James. She couldn't believe she could see him.

"But, but, you're in heaven not the other side, aren't you?" Ladle said.

"They did it, Ladle. Our children and all the moon witches have portals set up. They are connected now, and as long as the moon, sun, and Star Witches continue to connect, the heavens dimension will be open to the most powerful," James explained as his voice echoed through the room.

Ladle smiled and walked closer to James.

"If the moon isn't out during the day, something is wrong, and the connection isn't there anymore," he explained.

"Okay, I understand. But why? Why are you still gone after so many things have changed?" Ladle asked.

James didn't want to tell her it was the lunar moon power, but he also never lied to her.

"I love you, Ladle Marie Amar, with all of my heart," James said.

Ladle smiled, tears running down her face. James walked over and wiped them away.

"I'll see you again. You know that, right?" James whispered.

"But this is different. You can't be reborn with me, James. This is it," Ladle cried.

"Our children are the most powerful witches who created a multiverse." James smiled, holding Ladle's cheek. "They will find a way that we can always be together."

Ladle still had doubts but saw how James truly believed that.

"They are still children. Just wait. As they grow, they will find and prepare such a spell for us," James said.

She held his face right back and kissed him. As they pulled apart, James saw Ladle was devastated.

"This is just the beginning of the end," he said.

Ladle smiled and wiped her tears. Just as James was about to fade away, he told her one last thing. "Your parents are home and never died. I left two rings with you if you decide you want them to remember their death or leave it be," James said as he gestured to the coffee table.

Two rings appeared on the table.

He disappeared as Ladle held the rings and squeezed them tight, wondering what she should do. Still holding them, she walked over to the window. Looking up to the sky, she saw parallel to the sun was the moon, shining bright, side by side.

***

~ 19 ~

DIVIDED TOGETHER

Rene and Anthony ended up in Sef's old room in the school basement. They couldn't give him a ring because he was not from this universe. They were hoping there was some sort of magic and miracle, so he still could remember the university and all he had done for the school.

As they were about to leave, Anthony noticed a picture lying on the floor. Rene asked him what it was as he picked it up. On each side of the long hallway were metal bar doors. Rene thought about it and walked closer to see the picture.

"Does this look like jail cells to you?" she asked.

"Yeah, definitely," Anthony said, shaking his head yes.

"I remember Sef mentioning a hidden jail cell a while back," Rene explained.

"Yeah, but the timeline changed. He wasn't here. Look at this room. No one has been down here," Anthony said. The bed was gone, one that Sef used to sleep on. His tools weren't there and different cleaning supplies were laid out in a disorganized manner, unlike how Sef used to keep things.

"Then why is this picture here?" Rene asked.

The two looked at the picture and then at each other.

A knock was heard at the door. Anthony put the picture in his pocket.

"Hey, you two, are you both okay?" Tulin asked, holding his finger where his new tattoo set in.

"Yes, thank you. We're fine. Just reminiscing is all," Rene said.

"He was a good friend," Tulin said. Silence filled the room.

"The new buildings guy, well, not new to him, he's been here the whole time. He'll be down here soon to check the water system."

The two nodded and followed Tulin upstairs. To their surprise, the whole school started clapping in their honor. They knew Tulin had something to do with this. Anthony and Rene smiled and took a bow.

Rene whispered in Anthony's ear, "I'm sure the others didn't get this sort of honor, but they should too."

Anthony nodded in agreement and raised his fist. Rene followed.

"This is for the complete moon power witches!" Anthony shouted. Everyone cheered.

"The Sun and Star deserve the same. It goes without saying we are in this together!" Rene shouted. They cheered again while Tulin couldn't be more proud.
***

On planet Earth, in a small village in Congjiang, there was a tower, and inside that very tower, the fire was out. At that very moment, clapping and cheering wasn't just on Altair. There was again a fire, which meant that the moon witches from all phases were back. The villagers cheered and cheered.

One man ran to a house not far from the tower.

He rushed inside and shook his head. Everyone in the room turned to see the baby - the first born since the fire returned. The parents looked at their child and smiled, naming her Hui.
***

Vannessa was seen holding hands with Colin. Rene couldn't help but smile.

"Come on, you two, our Covens are joining forces," Rene said. All wearing the rings, both Rene and Anthony's covens stood side by side.

That night, Rene pulled Vannessa to the side.

"I need you to come with me," Rene said.

"You just got back? Where to now?" Vannessa asked.

"I have to do one more thing and it involves Max," Rene said. Vannessa knew exactly what she wanted to do.

Rene and Vannessa used the coven's power to arrive on Cassini, not far from Max's house. Rene held onto what Blair gave her to reverse the spell she used with the hydra's blood. Vannessa cringed because it looked disgusting, but Rene had to drink it and make the reverse spell. She took a deep breath and chugged the potion. After a couple seconds, she spoke out loud the wish she desired.

"Did it work?" Vannessa asked.

Rene walked toward Max's door. She stopped at the gate and took another deep breath. Vannessa watched as Rene was able to make it to the door. She knocked.

Max felt a strange energy that made him eager to run to that door. Rene and Max looked at each other face to face. He smiled and hugged her. She saw him wearing the ring right away and knew her siblings were already there.

"What's that smell?" Max asked.

Rene held her mouth as Vannessa laughed a few feet away.

"I had to drink something disgusting in order to reverse the spell," Rene answered.

"Um, there was no spell," Max said.

Vannessa laughed so loud she started crying.

"In this timeline, I didn't do a damn spell! I just drank that for no reason!" Rene shouted. "How did I get this potion then? It was given to lift this very spell I put on us."

"Ah, now I get what Molly was saying," Max said as Rene's face turned red.

"Molly?"

"Yeah, I believe that might have been pickles and sour patch kids blended together."

Rene was already thinking of revenge for her annoying little sister. She held it together.

"Well, I know you are aware of what I did even if it didn't happen," she said, pointing to the ring on his finger. "I'm sorry I did that to us."

Max told her it was okay when a girl came up behind him. He remembered the history he and Rene had, but some things had changed. Rene knew this memory she had with Max did, in fact, change.

At first, it was silent when the girl walked up to the door. Max quickly realized the silence and introduced his girlfriend to Rene.

Vannessa stopped laughing and watched, wondering how Rene would react.

"I'm happy for the both of you. That's awesome you found someone," she said with a smile.

"Is that Rene I hear?" Julie came out and hugged Rene. "We will never forget the memories we had with you and your family! You are always welcome here. That will never change."

Max nodded in agreement as his girlfriend smiled. It seemed like he wanted to say more as Rene started walking away. Julie asked his girlfriend to please help her with the turkey in the kitchen. When they walked off, Max ran toward Rene.

"I will always care about you no matter what, okay?"

Rene smiled. "Same." They hugged before Max ran back inside.

Rene and Vannessa walked away from the home.

"I'm one of the strongest witches out there, and yet my stupid younger sister can still trick me?" Rene asked.

"Well, you guys have to piece together the changes of both timelines." Vannessa laughed. "Molly took advantage of that and knew that if you still saw the potion sitting there, then that meant you were given it because the spell still happened."

"Yeah, I see that now," Rene said, holding out her hands to Vannessa.

"After all, she has the same amount of power as you do. I don't see that being a good thing." Vannessa laughed.

Just as they were about to leave holding hands, Brenda flew over to them.

"Hi," she said as she landed on her feet gently.

"Hey, Brenda," Rene said. Vannessa smiled.

"Can you tell Austin to please come visit or maybe just say hi?" she said hesitant about what she wanted to tell him. "No, tell him to never forget me, or you know what? Tell him if he is a decent person to reach out." Rene and Vannessa couldn't help but look at each other and smile. "No, maybe, that's too cruel. Never mind. If he wanted to see me again, he would...right?"

"Are you finished, love?" Rene said.

"Yes, sorry."

"No need to apologize. You are a beautiful and wise young lady. Wise beyond your years. Please do not wait for a man because if he isn't the one, then you missed your chance on others who might have been your true love. If it's meant to be, it will be. I know that sounds cliché, but it's true. I will tell him you said hi and let the path take its course."

Brenda smiled. It was a broken smile, but she nodded and said thank you.

Vannessa looked at Rene disgusted. "Weren't you raised around Humans?"

"Yes, why?"

Brenda started to rise and fly away.

"Doesn't seem like it," Vannessa pointed out.

Rene thought about it.

"Wait, Brenda! Screw it. I'll tell him to get his booty over here and see you again! In my opinion, you two looked so cute together!" Rene shouted.

Brenda smiled and flew away.

"That's more like it." Vannessa laughed.

"Yeah, well, I saw it in her eyes, her soul. It wasn't the eyes of his soulmate," Rene said.

Vannessa was shocked. "Shit, then why did you say that?"

"Because growing up around humans taught me that love, breakups, and everything in between are all part of life. Memories and experiences—without it all, it's way too boring."

Upon Rene and Vanessa's return, they immediately went to the university, where Anthony was delivering a speech. He declared his determination to fight for Altair and fulfill his father's wish to become a leader of the magic knights.

As Rene observed her brother, she realized that he had chosen the path of a soldier over reuniting with Serenity, his soulmate. Despite knowing that Serenity was meant for him, Anthony's obligations as a knight left no room for her. Rene was unwilling to let her brother neglect his feelings for Serenity. She approached him and stood by his side, vowing to fight alongside him. Although she hoped that Anthony and Serenity would eventually cross paths again, she understood that his duty as a knight came first.

Rene grasped her brother's hand tightly and raised it up for all to see. In the midst of the crowd, she spotted Finn, a member of her coven, and Vanessa, who smiled warmly at her while gesturing toward Finn. Rene felt a rush of joy, knowing that Finn was devoted to standing by her side no matter what challenges they faced—even if it meant battling in a conflict. As long as they had each other, they would always stick together.
***

After graduation, Molly and Isabel both received their diplomas on stage. Isabel noticed Elijah waiting for her in the audience. Ever since they returned to this new timeline, the two had been in communication. As Isabel walked off the stage, she knew she and Elijah would be staying on Earth to help humanity navigate the future together.

When humanity evolved, Isabel and Elijah would guide them to enlightenment.

Whenever the crescent moon shined its light, humans could catch a glimpse of the enchanting portal that was coming, but through time and space, had always been waiting for them.

As the group chatted, Isabel caught sight of Ryan at the back of the gathering. Her smile was returned by his. Elijah followed her gaze, but Ryan had already disappeared. Isabel realized that he had kept his promise to attend the graduation ceremony.

Molly's friends cheered her on as she received her diploma. Danny hugged her and exclaimed that he never wanted to attend school again despite his immortality. This caused Molly to burst out laughing, and her family joined in. As Molly ran toward Beyron, he picked her up and asked about her plans. She turned to Danny and excitedly announced that the three of them should go on a road trip—but with a magical twist. Beyron was intrigued and asked her to explain. Molly explained that with the insane number of planets in the universe, she had a burning desire to see them all.

Beyron, Molly, and Danny agreed to travel not only on planet Earth but also throughout the galaxy.

Austin sat there watching everyone decide their next adventure. After the ceremony, he traveled alone to New Orleans looking for Amanda.

"Austin?" she said, seeing him first.

"Amanda!"

"What are you doing back so soon?" she asked.

"Remember that potion I gave you?"

"Yeah, why?"

"Well, I didn't say anything before because everyone was here, but, um, I heard what you were thinking about using it for."

"I want to be human again. A witch will be fine, just not a monster-looking wolf," she explained.

"My siblings all have plans, even my mom does, and for a while, I kept thinking about mine. My mom said since I'm the only one younger than eighteen I need to be with her. But I'm a warlock—a powerful one at that."

Amanda looked curious about why he was telling her this.

"Are you happy here?" Austin asked.

"I mean…." She thought about it.

"Come with me. Bring your pack, too," Austin said.

"Where?"

"Back to your home. I made up my mind. I'm going to meet up with Graham in Cassini."

Amanda smiled and quickly agreed.

Austin remembered what Rene told him about Brenda, but a part of him felt connected to Amanda. And he couldn't ignore that. He knew he would see Brenda there, but after all, he was still a teenager. Two girls crushing on him? Why not.

Amanda wanted to make peace with Graham and unite their families. She believed in making her own choices and not being held responsible for her parents.
***

Austin went home to talk to his mom. She understood everything and knew he would be just fine. Julie, of course, wasn't far from Graham's family's land, so when Austin went upstairs to pack, she quickly sent communication to Julie to keep an eye out for her boy.

Although Ladle was returning to her parents, she was once again going to be separated from her children by just one tree. However, this time around, her children were aware of their abilities and had retained all their memories. Despite their young age, their minds were brimming with knowledge, and their powers were truly out of this world.

~ 20 ~

WHAT'S NEXT

While traveling through space in a spacecraft designed by Susie that could travel for hundreds of years, Molly unexpectedly found herself traveling without intending to.

Fire was everywhere, buildings destroyed, dead bodies under the rubble. *The Sun Witch agreed to peace,* Molly thought. *What the heck happened to this planet?*

While looking for answers, she came across what looked like a newspaper stand in the gravel and attempted to locate a specific date. It was the year 2027, and as she continued searching for any signs of life, she stumbled upon Kevin's lifeless body on the ground. At that moment, it dawned on her that she was no longer in her own universe.

Moving fast toward him, with her heart pounding in anticipation, she soon realized that he was long gone. Her eyes looked as if she raged with anger. Without hesitation, she was on another mission to save Kevin and find out who had done this.

Kevin and the Crescent Moon Werewolves embark on a new adventure as they try to save another universe created by the Witches.

In Kevin's universe, the witches' darkness that spread throughout the multiverse had taken on a monstrous form in their minds and could even manifest in reality with a single thought of it. This thing caused a deadly disease that threatened millions of people worldwide. Kevin knew that the moon witches could not save them because he was beyond their universe.

The adventure continues. Kevin and The Crescent Wolves have a story to tell; they hold the power to mold the fate of their world.